THE RETURN OF
LORD RUTHVEN

also by Frank J. Morlock

Lord Ruthven the Vampire
(*John William Polidori,
Charles Nodier and Eugène Scribe*)

THE RETURN OF LORD RUTHVEN

by
Alexandre Dumas

adapted in English by
Frank J. Morlock

A Black Coat Press Book

Acknowledgements: We are indebted to Jackie Stanton for typing the plays, Conrad Cady for publishing them and supporting my work for several years, and David McDonnell for proofreading the typescript.

Dedicated to my grandchildren, Miranda, Melissa, Alexis, Miles and Nicholas.

Visit our website at www.blackcoatpress.com

Table of Contents

Introduction
The Dark Side of Alexandre Dumas

I believe that most fans of Alexandre Dumas *père* (1802-1870) think of the great French author as the ebullient, buoyant and exciting writer of adventures such as *The Three Musketeers* (1844), *The Count of Monte-Cristo* (1845-46), *The Man in The Iron Mask* (1848-50) and many more.[1]

But in fact, Dumas has a dark side, present even in his sword-swinging romps. Milady murders callously in *The Three Musketeers* and the story ends with her being beheaded. (The executioner is, in fact, the brother of her former lover, who was himself executed for thefts that she committed.) Rather tough stuff, when you think of it.

Dumas wrote *Le Vampire* in 1851. The Dumas version of Lord Ruthven is a much more formidable night-stalker than Charles Nodier's somewhat effeminate creation.[2] Finely attuned to the trends and popular fashions of the literary marketplace, Dumas capitalized on the success of the French translations of E.T.A. Hoff-

---

[1] Alexandre Dumas *fils* (1824-1895) was Dumas' illegitimate son, whose care and education were nevertheless unflaggingly supported by his father. Dumas *fils* gained fame with his 1847 novel *La Dame aux Camélias*, a.k.a. *Camille*, which inspired Giuseppe Verdi's 1853 opera, *La Traviata*.

[2] Presented in *Lord Ruthven the Vampire*, Black Coat Press, 2004. Throughout these books, for the sake of consistency, we have chosen the spellings of *Ruthven* (with a *v* instead of a *w*) and *vampire* (with a *i* instead of a *y*). (*Note from the Publisher*.)

mann's *Tales* and *The Thousand and One Nights* to write a number of other plays and novels that, like *Le Vampire*, dealt with occult themes.

Dumas wrote more vampire stories as part of a mammoth collection entitled *Les Mille et Un Fantômes* (1849), variously and incompletely published in English as *Horror at Fontenay* and *The White Lady*. There are two stories in that collection that essentially follow the same pattern as *Le Vampire*; in one, a pair of brothers are involved, in the other, the eponymous White, or Pale, Lady, is a female vampire.

In 1857, Dumas turned to the depiction of another monster and, with *The Wolf Leader*, penned one of the first, modern werewolf stories–and still one of the best. A supernatural thriller set in the 17th century in Dumas' home town, *The Wolf Leader* tells the story of Thibault, a young shoemaker who is nearly beaten to death by evil noblemen and makes a pact with some kind of demon-wolf. The demon offers Thibault the power to harm anyone he wishes, but the more evil acts he commits, the more he starts turning into a wolf himself and becoming the leader of a pack of killer wolves.

Another historical novella *Urbain Grandier* (1841; dramatized in 1850) deals with the notorious case of "Devils of Loudon" in the mid-1600s. Grandier is a soldier turned monk on the death of his betrothed. Unbeknownst to him, his fiancée is, in reality, being held prisoner in a dungeon beneath a convent by the Mother Superior who was once Grandier's lover. Grandier learns the truth by means of his younger brother. The youth can be placed in a trance and, when in such a trance, he is able to see events at a distance, and has "seen" that his brother's betrothed is in fact alive. This is a very precise description of what, in modern ESP terminology, is described as "remote viewing." This is the only supernatural element in the play, although Grandier is convicted of witchcraft and satanism.

Dumas carried this a step further in *The Corsican Brothers* (1844; dramatized 1850) where it is a tradition in a Corsican family that, when one brother is about to die, his astral body appears to the survivor. This short novel became a famous play, that is still being performed today. It was thought, at the time, that it gained much of its power from the normality of the story's other events. It made the existing world seem so much more real. (One has heard similar remarks applied to Stephen King's works.)

In a later, and one of his best, novels *Joseph Balsamo Dumas* (a.k.a. *Memoirs of a Physician*), Dumas deals at great length with Cagliostro. In that novel, the famed Magi uses his occult powers to bring down the French Monarchy and start the Revolution. Balsamo also uses the mediumistic powers of a young virgin to master "distant viewing" and thus pave the way for the destruction of the Monarchy. Balsamo returned as Cagliostro in its sequel, *The Queen's Necklace* (1849).

Isaac Laquedem (1853) was Dumas' own version of Eugène Sue's *The Wandering Jew* (1844-45) and it, too, happily mixed occult conspiracies and historical events.

Dumas had a strong interest in, and knowledge of, the Occult. One of his earliest plays, *The Alchemist* (1839), was a collaboration with Gérard de Nerval. Earlier in his career, Dumas had also penned *Castle Eppstein* (1843) and *Le Trou d'Enfer* (*The Mouth of Hell*; 1851)—two *romans noirs* in which Gothic plots were used; in the former, the protagonist's mother is a spectral figure, half-dead, half-alive. As the translator of that story notes in her introduction, Gothic stories usually involved a pure creature in love with a demon lover–or a vampiric one!

Dumas also wrote, or translated, a German Fate drama, *February 24*, in which a young man returns to his impoverished mountain home in Switzerland only to be murdered by his parents who do not recognize him. There are no supernatural creatures in that play, but everything revolves around the near-mystic anniversary date of February 24, when 20 years before, the hero quarreled with his father and left. February 24 was also the day when, during the Revolution, the mob stormed the palace of Versailles and took the King and the Royal family hostage to Paris. The son was a member of the notorious Swiss Guards, many of whom were killed defending the King on that fateful day. Probably one of Dumas' grimmest stories, it was initially so unpopular that a happy ending was tacked on, but it has, apparently, not survived.

While not exactly an occult element, Dumas repeatedly returned to the theme of mistaken identities and false imprisonment in his works. The victim may have no idea why he is being imprisoned, like the hapless Edmond Dantes in *The Count of Monte-Cristo*. Or he may be imprisoned simply for being who he is, and the resemblance he bears to his twin brother the King as in *The Man in The Iron Mask*. Both seem to be a variation of the fear of being buried alive, a theme not uncommon in the works of many writers of the 19th century. In one of the stories in *Les Mille et Un Fantômes*, Dumas suggests that life might continue for a time after being guillotined.

Revenge played a big role in many of Dumas' plays and novels. *The Count of Monte-Cristo* is considered to be one of the best revenge novels ever written. Once Dantes escapes, he returns as the fabulously rich eponymous Count to undo the trio of men who, from jealousy, destroyed his life. But it plays a strong part in the sequel to *The Three Musketeers*, *Twenty Years After* (1845), where Milady's son, the evil Mordaunt, returns to hunt down the men he believes responsible for his mother's death. That she was guilty of murder means nothing to him; she was his mother. (Additionally, Dumas adapted *Hamlet* into French, another great revenge play.)

Although it was Victor Hugo, not Dumas, who wrote a play about Lucrezia Borgia, Dumas dealt at length with the Borgias in his *Celebrated Crimes* nonfiction series (1839-41). The second wife of Villefort in *The Count of Monte-Cristo* is a poisoner, as is Milady in *The Three Musketeers*. He seems to have a particular horror of them, mixed with a strange fascination towards evil deeds in general.

In *The Mohicans of Paris* (1854-59), which transplanted James Fenimore Cooper's convoluted intrigue into the Parisian Underworld of the 19th century, a previously decent man is persuaded by his mistress, Ursula, to kill his niece and nephew in order to gain a huge inheritance from his brother. The plan miscarries, but the horrible plot is described in exquisite detail, and it leads to other crimes and mysteries. Here, Dumas invents a character, Monsieur Jackal, who is a Police Inspector of great abilities, probably modeled on the real-life Vidocq, the famous French criminal turned Head of the Sûreté. Jackal fights the mysterious and heroic "Salvator," who is the leader of a Revolutionary conspiracy. Jackal and Salvator anticipate Paul Féval's Gregory Temple and

11

Jean Diable from *John Devil* (1862),[3] Victor Hugo's Javert from *Les Misérables* (1862) and Emile Gaboriau's Monsieur Lecoq (1866), all precursors of the greatest detective of all, Sherlock Holmes.

Then, there is *La Tour de Nesle* (1832), a play about Queen Marguerite de Bourgogne who had her lovers brought to an isolated tower near the Louvre for a tryst; afterwards, for her security, these men were killed and their bodies thrown into the Seine. Eventually, she wound up killing one of her own sons by an early lover, after having had sexual relations with him...

Grisly executions are commonplace in Dumas' works. In *La Reine Margot* (1845), he introduces a very kindly man who is, in fact, the Executioner of Paris. He winds up executing the hero. Then, there is the Executioner of Bethune in *The Three Musketeers*, who beheads Milady; he in turn is murdered in the sequel by Mordaunt, posing as a priest giving him the last rites after hearing his confession.

In recent years, much has been made of the role of the Priory of Sion; speculative articles and books have been published, some actually involving quite good research. The Priory, supposedly founded by Leonardo Da Vinci, had later leaders that included Dumas' friend and close mentor, Charles Nodier. After Nodier's death, he was succeeded by Victor Hugo, another close friend if sometimes rival of Dumas.

We have been unable to discover if Dumas was a member of, or closely associated with, the notorious Priory, but he certainly seemed to know about it. In *Les Companions of Jehu* (1857), members of the eponymous Anti-Republican, Anti-Bonapartist secret society take

---

[3] *John Devil* is scheduled to be published by Black Coat Press.

refuge in an abandoned "Priory of *Siom*." The substitution of *Siom* for *Sion* hardly conceals the true identity of Priory. Additionally, in his play, *Caligula* (1837), Dumas recounts the story that, after the Crucifixion, Mary-Magdalene landed as a refugee in France and lived a holy life in a cave. Considering when the play was written, it would seem that Dumas must have heard that story, a key belief of the Priory, either from Hugo or Nodier. There may be more, but these tantalizing bits of information will probably never be fully elucidated.

All in all, one should not be surprised by the fact that Alexandre Dumas *père* was interested in vampires, or by the skill with which he handled the theme.

Frank J. Morlock

The Return of Lord Ruthven

by
Alexandre Dumas

adapted in English
by
Frank J. Morlock

Characters in the Play

Lord Ruthven, the Vampire
Ziska, the Ghoul, a Moorish-looking woman
Count Gilbert de Tiffauges
Helen de Tiffauges, his sister
Juana de Torillas, a Spanish noblewoman
Antonia, Gilbert's beloved
Juan Rozo, a Spanish hotelier
Petra Rozo, his daughter
Botaro, Petra's intended husband
Lazare, a Spanish servant
First Traveler, Count Gilbert's companion
Second Traveler, Count Gilbert's companion
Third Traveler, Count Gilbert's companion
Jarwick, a servant at Tiffauges
Lahennee, another servant at Tiffauges
Melusina, the fairy
First Peasant Girl
Second Peasant Girl
A Bohemian, a gypsy
An Old Man
A Peasant
A Servant
Peasants, Travelers, Fisherman, etc.

Act I

Scene I

The court of a Spanish Inn. Battlements on the left, the right a large grilled gate giving on the roadway. Mountains in the background.

At Rise, the court offers a very animated aspect. Men, women and children are arriving and greeted affectionately. A Bohemian sings to the accompaniment of his mandolin. They dance to the refrain with the sound of castanets. People are everywhere at windows, gates and on the tops of walls.

BOHEMIANS AND PEASANTS
(Chorus)
In the bowers,
In the green grass
Dance girls!
Dance boys!

A BOHEMIAN
I was on the way from Huesias
My heart was heavy
My step was slow
Guitar on my back
But my lips were silent
Because everyone is quiet
By the ruins of Tormenar

BOHEMIANS
(Refrain by Chorus)
A Traveler passes by
"What castle is this
Gigantic, knifelike,
Mr. Mandolin Man?
Is it the alcazar?"
"No, señor–
It's the ruins of Tormenar."
(Refrain by Chorus)
What living soul dwells in the castle?
By day–the terrified
And by night, the dead.
–Hey Mr. Mandolin Man
I am late
Come sleep in the ruins
Of Tormenar!
(Refrain by Chorus)

Juan Rozo, Petra, Botaro and Lazare enter.

ROZO
Come on, come on, enough of dances and songs
like that. Get out–all the vagabonds–beggars and
gypsies. We won't have enough room here, even
after you get out.

The courtyard empties little by little.

LAZARE
The fact is, I don't know how Father Rozo will
be able to lodge everyone.

ROZO

Come, children, put your mules in the stable—
give the porter your baggage and come embrace
the kids.

BOTARO

Say, father-in-law—it seems to me your house
can't possibly hold our two families.

ROZO

Bah! We've lodged as many as fifty Christians
here at one time—they all ate and slept under my
roof.

LAZARE

Yes, but the next day, you should have heard
them. The fifty Christians swore like a hundred
pagans.

BOTARO

Ah, yes—fifty ate and slept with you? Good,
then! But look here father-in-law—there are
sixty-seven of us. After this, a night is soon
over, right? And sure, the bride must be well
brought to bed.

LAZARE
        (aside)
Egoist!

BOTARO
Why, by the way, father-in-law—

ROZO
What?

BOTARO
Suppose some travelers arrive?

ROZO
Well?

BOTARO
What will you do?

ROZO
I will say that there is no more room and they
will go away.

BOTARO
Still, an innkeeper...

ROZO
The day my daughter is married, there is no
more inn. That day, the house is mine–too bad
about the travelers! They were free to come
yesterday and they are free to come tomorrow.
Those who are here already, it goes without
saying I won't   put them out the door. So we
have a Moorish lady. Well, I'll keep her
although she doesn't spend much. She only eats
a few grains of rice and so comically–like this,
with two little ivory sticks.

LAZARE
I am sure that she gets up at night to eat olla

LAZARE (cont'd)
podrida and gazpacho since it is impossible
that a human creatures lives on three or four
grains of rice a day.

BOTARO
Father-in-law, we are counting just now sixty-
seven people in the house.

ROZO
Yes—everyone understands.

BOTARO
Including the scullions?

ROZO
Including the scullions.

BOTARO
Well, we were mistaken—we are only sixty-six.

ROZO
Ha! Ha!—Who's leaving?

BOTARO
You forget that we agreed.

ROZO
What?

BOTARO
(pointing to Lazare)
That this comedian Lazare—

ROZO

Ah, yes, Lazare.

BOTARO

Leave the house.

ROZO

It's true.

LAZARE

(aside)

Decidedly it's about me. I believe the groom is asking Señor Rozo to take me to his service–that won't go with the husband, but it will go well with the wife's side.

BOTARO

(to Rozo)

In love and a piggish eater.

ROZO

Piggish eater–I don't say–but in love–are you really sure?

BOTARO

Listen, father-in-law–you know it was agreed, that he would leave the day of my wedding. I have your word–he's got to go.

ROZO

Oh well, since you absolutely insist.

BOTARO

Absolutely!

24

ROZO

I am going to invite him to pack his bags. Come here, Lazare.

LAZARE

Me?

ROZO

Yes, you.

BOTARO
(to Petra)
Turn your head the other way, my wife.

ROZO
(looking for Lazare)
Hey, where'd you go?

LAZARE
(who has gone to the large gate)
Over here! Don't you see?

ROZO

Travelers. There's no more room.

Enter a man and a woman followed by three children.

LAZARE

You here–the boss say there's no more room–you can go away–huh? What?–Ah, damn it's true.

ROZO

What are they saying?

LAZARE

They say that they are man and wife and three little children–that they've been a long way today and that, if they have to continue their way, they will die of fatigue.

ROZO

That's possible, but there's no room.

LAZARE

They still say they'll be content with the least cover.

BOTARO

Look, father-in-law, give them the attic where this scapegrace Lazare lodges, since he is leaving.

ROZO

In fact, that's an idea–Lazare, escort them to your room–they will sleep there tonight.

LAZARE

Well, and me?

ROZO

You?

LAZARE

Yes–where will I bed down?

ROZO

You, Lazare, will sleep wherever you wish.

LAZARE

Well, in the stable?

ROZO

No.

LAZARE

In the kitchen then.

ROZO

No.

LAZARE

Yes, I understand, in the cellar. The devil–
I won't be hot in the cellar–hopefully there's a
certain little wine from Montello.

ROZO

No.

LAZARE

Not in the cellar either?

ROZO

Lazare, you won't lodge in this house tonight–
pack your bags and go.

LAZARE

You are kicking me out?

ROZO

It's my son-in-law who demands it.

LAZARE

And why's that?

ROZO

It appears you've been courting my daughter.

LAZARE

Me?–oh! How can they say that?

ROZO

It's Botaro who pretends that–and he must
know.

LAZARE

What! Señor Botaro–you pretend that I–?

BOTARO

That's fine–one knows what one knows–one
sees what one has seen.

LAZARE

Oh, because of one night that I was worn out
from husking, and Señora Petra was watching
me, he threw straw in her face, and I socked him
in the eye?

BOTARO

Good, good–enough.

LAZARE

Why ask her, your wife, if I embraced her–I bet
she'll say no.

ROZO

Look, look, your bill is paid–on your way.

LAZARE

And where do you want me to go?

BOTARO

What's that to me? On your way–

LAZARE

On my way without supper? But you owe me supper for today.

BOTARO

Some bread, some cheese and a fistful of olives and on your way!

LAZARE

Oh! Because today precisely–because it's a wedding super–with ragouts, roasts, pastry and sweets–because today, for the first time, there's a supper a bit fitting the house–they send me away–they kick me out. Fie, master Rozo–it's rather petty what you are doing–I never thought this of you!

ROZO

Listen, Botaro, he's a bit–right. It's a feast day and to make him eat his bread when the spits turn–heavens–that reminds me! I forgot to turn the spit. Great! The goose will be burned.

He runs out hurriedly.

BOTARO

It's fine—I agree to wait until you've dined.
Drink, eat, fill up like a cask, fill yourself to
overflowing like a goatskin but when the gates
close, you understand, try to be on the outside
rather than on the inside.

LAZARE

So be it! Let them go, Señor Botaro.

BOTARO
(to travelers)
Come this way, my friends. I will escort you to
your room.
(to Lazare)
Goodbye, Señor Glutton.

LAZARE

Goodbye, Señora Bride.

PETRA
(as she goes)
Poor Lazare.

They leave.

LAZARE
(alone)
Isn't it shameful to put a poor young man out the
door at night, in a desert, in the midst of
mountains, when all the malefactors take their
gambols on the highways and in the rocks—when
this black castle of Tormenar disgorges at

LAZARE (cont'd)

midnight, from its ruins, bats, vultures, owls and
serpents! And all this because I caught the eye of
a young girl. Oh, when I think that I will be all
alone on the highways and that, as I turn, I will
notice this same Castle Tormenar which watches
travelers from on high with its large windows
like staring eyes.

He notices Ziska the Mooress who passes in the back.

LAZARE

Heavens! The Arab girl who only eats rice.

A noise.

LAZARE

Now what's that?

They call Lazare.

LAZARE

Yes, call Lazare! Since I no longer belong to this
house, I won't reply.

They call again.

LAZARE

Go to the devil. Look–what's wrong? A mule
and muleteer? More travelers? No, a woman.
She's got here at the right moment.

Juana enters.

JUANA

In the midst of the whole world, won't I be able
to find someone to speak to?

LAZARE

To me, Señora, if you like.

JUANA

I am really in an inn–right, my friend?

LAZARE

In an inn where no one can stay, yes, Señora.

JUANA

No one can stay! Why?

LAZARE

Because the innkeeper is marrying his daughter–
Señorita Petra, a charming girl–whose eye one is
forbidden to catch.

JUANA

I have a service to ask of someone, and I pay
generously when people oblige me.

LAZARE

Speak Señora! You fall in luck–I am as free as
the air! An idea! You don't have a muleteer,
Señora, you must have need of a cook or a
valet–I have just such qualities, go!

JUANA

For the moment I need a guide, and that's all.

LAZARE

What luck you have, Señora—I run the errands
for the inn. There's not a step from here to
Huesias, not a stone, a heath, that I don't know.

JUANA

Good. Come.

LAZARE

Right away! For how long do you engage me,
Señora?

JUANA

Why, for the time I take to get to my destination.

LAZARE

Is the Señora going far? I am not curious. That's
a frightful sin—but to guide you, I think it is
necessary that I know where you are going.

JUANA

My friend, I am going to the Castle Tormenar.

LAZARE

Huh?

JUANA

Well? Didn't you hear me?

LAZARE

Did I hear you? I think so!

JUANA

Then, come.

LAZARE
Oh! No, no, Señora–I am not going.

JUANA
Why?

LAZARE
Because no one goes to the Castle Tormenar, Señora, because honest Christians don't mention that name.

JUANA
Look, I have business at the castle.

LAZARE
At a castle which is uninhabited, in ruins and which lodges only reptiles, which lodges nothing but ghosts–you have business there, Señora?

JUANA
My dear friend–I wanted to give a piastre to the guide–after what you've told me, I will give ten.

LAZARE
You can give a hundred–you can give a thousand, but I will never go to the Castle Tormenar.
(aside)
Who is this woman?–Brrr...

JUANA
Very well. I will find servants less disinterested than you–and much braver.

LAZARE

Try! You want me to help you try to find them?
You are going to see. Hey, ladies and gentlemen,
hey, Christians, hey, pagans, hey, everybody.

Running on all sides.

LAZARE

Here's a lady who needs a guide to run a little
errand and she's offering ten piastres, who wants
it?

ALL

Me! Me! Me!

LAZARE

Wait. The little errand leads to Castle Tormenar.

ALL

Oh!

LAZARE

Look–don't fight like that over who will go–it's
embarrassing to the lady.
        (to Juana)
Well–what did I tell you?

JUANA

        (aside)
My God! Why he's expecting me–he'll accuse
me–he'll think I've broken my word.

LAZARE

It must be pretty impossible for me not to go, since I can't stay an hour more here in this dump!

ROZO
(entering)
What were you saying, Lazare?

LAZARE

The boss!

JUANA

You are the master of this inn, Señor? You probably don't partake in all the superstitions. You will really find me a guide to go to Tormenar.

ROZO
To Tormenar! Holy Virgin!

BOTARO
To Tormenar! Jesus!

JUANA
I will go alone, then.

ROZO
Señora, don't do it! And anyway, you can't do it. The mules themselves will refuse to climb to that cursed castle.

JUANA
I will go on foot.

ROZO

Your little feet will be torn to shreds before you
get half-way there.

JUANA

Alas! Won't there pass on this road a man who
can oblige a poor woman?

LAZARE

Listen, Señora! Take me into your service and
tomorrow morning I will help you find a very
brave man who will lead you to Tormenar.
        (aside)
It will take at least a year to find him.

VOICE
        (from outside)
Hola! Hey!

BOTARO

Oh–father-in-law, can't they leave us in peace?

ROZO

Go see, Lazare, go explain to them.

LAZARE

Master Rozo, if I were still in your service,
I would hurry to obey you.

GILBERT
        (outside)
Hey there! Are you going to open?

ROZO

Who are you?

GILBERT

You see well enough, by God. I suppose we
don't have the air of robbers.

ROZO

My dear sir, if you were thieves, you'd see we
are here in sufficient numbers to receive you.

GILBERT

Well—since we are honest travelers and you in
there are lazybones with nothing to do—open the
gate for us.

LAZARE

This gentleman expresses himself very well,
doesn't he, Señora? A bit of an accent.

ROZO

Useless to open for you, Señor Traveler, there's
no more room in the inn.

GILBERT

What a joke! There are about a dozen of us—
eight gentlemen and four ladies who've formed
a little caravan to have more safety on the way—
twelve persons to lodge—what a big thing for
your inn which resembles a barracks!

BOTARO

Yes, Señor, twelve people are little but we are
already sixty-seven here.

LAZARE

Of which one's married.

GILBERT

Yes, ladies, they will open, don't worry,
Mr. Innkeeper! Hey! Little fellow down there–
come here a bit. These ladies observed to me
that the heavens are getting dark–and a storm
threatens and they have not the least intention of
spending the night outside.

LAZARE
(looking at the sky)
Not even the resource to say "under the pretty
stars!"

ROZO

These ladies will have to do the best they can,
my dear sir–but they won't enter here. We are
choked already. And then, I'm marrying my
daughter and we want to stay *en famille*. So,
good luck and go with God, Señor Traveler.

GILBERT

Ah! So it's like that? You don't want to open the
gate for us?

ROZO

Why, no–that's my right.

GILBERT

We must then remove your signboard which
hangs there at the end of the rope. Wait, I am
going to unhook it for you.

He shoots at it.

ROZO
Señor Gentleman!

BOTARO
You outrage the property.

LAZARE
I bet he's a Frenchman. Say, Señor Botaro, what
a nice shot, eh! If this gentleman fired at a man–
a man's much larger than a rope.

ROZO
Well, you leave, Señor? I am mayor as well as
innkeeper–do you know that?

GILBERT
Yes–but you are an innkeeper at the same time
you are mayor. Open this gate, once; twice–
thrice! No! Well, gentlemen, let's lay siege to
the house and break down these rotten boards.

ROZO
Why this is frightful!

BOTARO
Murder!

LAZARE
(to Botaro)
Say, Señor, here's one who will catch the eye of
our wife!

BOTARO

Shut up, servant!

ROZO

Why, let's defend ourselves! Let's chase them off!

BOTARO

Without weapons? These brigands have muskets and pistols.

LAZARE

And know how to use them! I wager as there are eight of them, they would kill fifteen men with the first volley.

ROZO

Mercy!

GILBERT

You won't open? To work!

ROZO

We are lost.

LAZARE

What fun not to belong to the house!

GILBERT

(breaking down the door)

Oh, the breach is made. Ladies take the trouble to enter. Come, gentlemen! Good day, dear innkeeper! Well, you see sixty-seven plus twelve only make seventy-nine.

LAZARE

It's incredible how much I like this traveler!
Oh—one more idea!

ROZO

I swear to you, Señor, that we have not one
corner, not one hole, not a niche which is free.
Count us, Señor, there's my daughter and my
son-in-law, whom I have the honor to present to
you. Here are my brothers, sisters, uncles, aunts.

GILBERT

Your cousins, your cousins and their families.
        (noticing the Moorish woman)
There's a strange face. Is she also of your
family?

ROZO

No, Señor, she's a Moorish lady who was
lodged here since yesterday, who we have not
disturbed as you will understand.

GILBERT

        (aside)
Somber face.

ZISKA

        (aside, eyes fixed on Gilbert)
He's handsome.

GILBERT

No space! Now, as you speak politely, we will
listen to you. No place, ladies! What to do?

GILBERT (cont'd)
Look, isn't there in the neighborhood some
house, another *posada*, a castle, even a shelter?

BOTARO
There's indeed a castle, Señor, but–

GILBERT
But what?

ROZO
Your five pistols, Señor Traveler, won't help
you to leave there safe and sound, even if you
change them into two big cannons.

GILBERT
Bah! What's in this castle? An ogre?

ROZO
I don't know what's there, Señor, but I know
whoever goes there never returns.

GILBERT
Come on!

ROZO
It was three years ago, a man wanted to spend
the night. They found him the next day–on the
rocks–head crushed, heart open–dead!

GILBERT
Ah!

ROZO

Last year, two captains from the garrison of Huesias went to Tormenar—that's the castle's name—from bravado, Señor. They slept side by side, a young man and an old man. The old man returned the next day, all pale, harmless, mad. He had, when he woke up, found his companion cold and dead in his arms with a gaping wound in the throat. Damn! It's true—everybody here saw it.

JUANA

My God!

LAZARE

I saw him buried. Brrr!

GILBERT

Well, there are robbers in that castle, by God— like in all your beautiful Spain.

ROZO

Señor Cavalier—the man from three years ago had his rings on his finger when they found his cadaver—and in the young captain from a year ago—they found his purse full—and wearing a very valuable medallion.

GILBERT

Say, gentlemen—you folks who are not from the country—does this frighten you a lot?

TRAVELER

Why's that, Count?

GILBERT

Because if you are no more afraid than I am, we
will go see Tormenar—it's Tormenar you said?
Sir, if they will crush the heads of all eight of
us—or slit our throats... Look—what do you think
of our army? We have sixteen pistols, eight
carbines, eight swords and enough ammunition
for a hundred shots. So shall we go to
Tormenar?

TRAVELER

Let's go to Tormenar!

LAZARE

The fools!
          (to Juana)
Say, Señora, it seems to me you've prettily done
your business and this is lucky.

JUANA

Yes.
          (to Gilbert)
Señor, Cavalier. A word, I beg you.

GILBERT

Ten, if you please, Señora.

JUANA

Would you listen to me for a moment privately?

GILBERT

At the end of the Earth, if that was agreeable to
you.

JUANA

Señor Cavalier–you are French and a gentleman.

GILBERT

My name is Gilbert de Tiffauges, I am a Breton
and an honest man, Madam.

JUAN

Sir, I have a service to ask of you. You are going
to Castle Tormenar?

GILBERT

Yes, Madame.

JUANA

I beg you to take me with you.

GILBERT

What! You are not frightened?

JUANA

With such brave men, Señor?

GILBERT

But you heard all the innkeeper said–

JUANA

I heard, I'm not afraid.

GILBERT

You are valiant, Madame–and we will be happy
to have an associate such as you. The charm of
your company will suffice, be sure of it–What

GILBERT (cont'd)

did the innkeeper say about the unlucky meeting
at Tormenar? It seems that, for me, the meeting
is not unlucky.

JUANA

Ah, Señor, it's the spirit of your nation which
takes things this way. You were speaking before
a language I understand better, and for you to
continue to treat me the same, I have only a
word to say to you, I am sure of it.

GILBERT

Speak, Madam.

JUANA

Count, I am Juana, the only child of the Marquis
de Torillas. My father put me in the convent of
the Annunciation at Huescas to prevent me from
marrying Don Luis de Figuerroa who I love and
to whom I am affianced before God. I received a
letter from Don Luis, which gave me a rendezvous in the mountains at Tormenar which he
must reach on his part through unfrequented
by-ways. I wrote Don Luis that wherever he will
go, I will go. Yesterday, I fled from the convent
with the aid of the Superior who is my friend
and I intend to rejoin my fiancé at Tormenar.
Then, we will go to the nearest port. It's to go in
safety to find Don Luis (who will thank you, sir)
that I beg you to take me with you to Tormenar.
Pure before God, I wish to be respected among
men–I've spoken to a loyal and courageous

JUANA (cont'd)

Cavalier–does he understand me? Can I hope he will fulfill my prayers?

GILBERT

Miss, I have, in Brittany, a sister that I love tenderly and who loves me with all the strength of her heart, a companion of my childhood, a friend put to every test–and I think her happy soon to be united with a brave gentleman of our country–but if she were to run some danger–or find herself in some embarrassment, I pray God she would meet a devotion as sincere, a protection as disinterested, a friendship as respectful as that I conjure you at this time to put to the proof. Deign to accept my arm, and it's not so much question as to merit the thanks of Don Luis as it is to be a tender brother to you and a solid support tonight, Miss. Don Luis will thank me, I give you my word! Come on, gentlemen–on the way to Tormenar!

JUANA

Be blessed, sir! I owe you my happiness.

LAZARE

My dear sir, you are really decided to leave for this castle?

GILBERT

Doubtless. Why this question?

LAZARE

Sir, I am looking for a master and you please me infinitely. I will willingly enter your service, but look here, if you go to Tormenar and you don't return, I shall have lost my situation before having got it. I will be the widow of my master–I want to spare myself that shame–and I will wait until tomorrow to see if you return from Tormenar. But from now on, regard me as your servant–you have made a famous acquisition.

GILBERT

My friend, I have no need of a servant–but if you absolutely wish to serve me, come! You draw back? You are a poltroon?

LAZARE

Me–a poltroon! Come on! I'm afraid of ghosts–that's all!

GILBERT

You are not my type–find another situation. I want whoever loves me to follow me everywhere–even to Hell.

LAZARE

You don't know what you are giving up.

Thunder.

GILBERT

Ah! Ah! The storm can be heard. It's invading the sky. Let's hurry, gentlemen! *En route* to the

GILBERT (cont'd)
terrible castle. But to have a solid spirit we must
fortify our stomachs. Master innkeeper, Señor
Mayor!

ROZO
My dear sir?

GILBERT
You don't have enough room–but you have lots
of chickens, partridges and rabbits, and lots of
veal and stuffed fish. Fill us a hamper of all
these good things–load a mule with old wine, we
will pay, we who do not have the ill luck to be
ghosts.

ROZO
Why, it's our supper, sir.

BOTARO
Father-in-law, let's eat less but get rid of these
noisy guests.

ROZO
(to his servants)
Obey this gentleman.

GILBERT
Marquis d'Hecquerey, Chevalier Marini and you
gentlemen, be the advanced guard. You others in
the center, with the ladies. We will be the rear
guard. Well, you, Señora?

JUANA

Order, sir.

LAZARE

What a shame! They are going to their death.
But what a supper they'll have first.

GILBERT

You are sure, Miss, that Don Luis de Figuerroa
has arrived first and that he's waiting for you?

JUANA

My letter sets the rendezvous for eight o'clock–
it's nine.

GILBERT
(to Rozo)
How long to get to the castle?

ROZO

An hour and a half, or two hours if you walk
behind the mules.

GILBERT

This is a promenade and we will arrive before
the rain. Come on, Señora, in an hour and a half
I will render my account to your handsome
fiancé. Goodbye, Señor Mayor–goodbye all.

ALL

Goodbye! Goodbye!

LAZARE

To think that in two hours, all these people will
perhaps have their necks broken!

ROZO

Let's go to supper.

ALL

Let's go to supper.

ZISKA

(aside, watching Juana)
You need two hours to find your handsome
fiancé. I will have joined him in three minutes.

She disappears.

CURTAIN.

Act II

Scene II

The castle of Tormenar–a huge hall of columns still solid, with large ruined windows through which one perceives the storm beginning to threaten. Side doors and doors at the rear. Old portraits with worm-eaten frames. Gothic furniture. An immense chimney that is surmounted by sculptured armorial bearings.

At Rise, Ziska hurriedly leaves a room at the right. She shuts the door after having taken a long look inside. Eleven o'clock sounds on a distant clock.

ZISKA
He was young! He was beautiful! I've become young and beautiful again.

The voice of travelers who, during the end of the storm, climb the rocks of Tormenar.

GILBERT
(outside)
This way, Señora–over here! There, good. Just two more steps.

ZISKA
Till next year–Gilbert.

She flies out the window.

Gilbert enters with the travelers.

> **GILBERT**
> Well–why here's a magnificent dining room!
> Come in, Señora. Come, gentlemen, enter,
> ladies.

> **FIRST TRAVELER**
> Ah, really superb.

> **SECOND TRAVELER**
> Oh! What a beautiful chimney! Look–nothing is
> lacking.

> **THIRD TRAVELER**
> Except a fire.

> **GILBERT**
> Fire? We're going to have one in an instant.
> Wood isn't rare here and our servants must have
> matches. Come in, all of you! The old doors and
> the old furniture will serve as logs and candles.
> Come here, in the middle–provisions–Aha!–but
> those imbeciles said we would find nothing in
> the castle? On the contrary, there's everything–
> even some tables.

The servants bring in the provisions. Some fix the table,
light candles, others start a fire.

> **GILBERT**
> Famous table, my word! The twelve peers may
> have had a longer table, but they didn't have one
> any more solid.

GILBERT (cont'd)
(to Juana)
Ah, pardon, Señora, I am always forgetting your
sadness, or rather I remember it and would like
to lessen it.

JUANA
You heard eleven o'clock strike as we entered
the castle.

GILBERT
Yes.

JUANA
Well, Don Luis still hasn't got here!

GILBERT
Oh, as for that, there's no need to worry. The
roads are atrocious. The storm has made the
ravines into quagmires. Dozen though we were,
it was all we could do to escape them. Think
how much trouble a lone traveler would have.

JUANA
Oh, I was also thinking of that. Even with terror.

GILBERT
Relax. Besides, Don Luis probably won't come
alone. He will be accompanied by some
domestic.

JUANA

Our secret isn't one that one confides in
strangers, no–Don Luis will have told no one.
Don Luis will come alone.

GILBERT

So much the better. That proves Don Luis is a
resolute, strong, clever, chevalier. Besides,
anyone you have chosen, Señora, cannot be an
ordinary man.

JUANA

Don Luis is brave and wears a valiant sword–but
there are perils which cannot be combated with
a sword.

GILBERT

What! You Miss, you, so courageous just now
against the wind, against the lightning, against
the thunder, against very real dangers–now you
let yourself go before chimeras?

JUANA

Señor Gilbert, pardon what I am going to say to
you–perhaps my heart no longer has the
strength. Fatigue and storm have exhausted it–
perhaps I am giving in to a premonition which
obsesses me, but then I was resolved, ardent,
happy while we were on the road, when I
believed I would see Don Luis–but now I am
beaten, inert, saddened by the time that it now is.

GILBERT

But it was only an instant ago that you were
laughing in my arms—in the mountains, when the
mule that carried our provisions was dragged by
the current, threatening, in reverse, the miracle
of Cana, to change our wine into water!

JUANA

Yes, it's true, but for several minutes—actually
from the moment I set foot over the sill of
this castle, I felt cold fear invade my entire
being. I dare not come forward. I dare not look
around me. I dare not sit down. I dare not, or
rather I cannot breathe—I am like one of those
wretched birds that pecking for grain, fall into
the trap of a cage—it even seems to me that, by
pronouncing a word, taking a step, risking a
gesture, I will create some overwhelming
misfortune that will fall on my head!

GILBERT

Oh, Señora, I curse these black walls, since they
inspire such ideas in you. Come on, look—some
courage! Look them in the face. A little humid,
it's true, hung with a great number of spider
webs, I confess, but in the end, honest walls
which, now, from the light of candles, the heat
of a good fire, the swell of a good supper and the
noise of plates and glasses—noises to which
they've long been unaccustomed, are going
to brighten up, make merry, revive—and you
won't see anything but gay echoes and
hospitable omens. Come on, come on! Sit down
and get rid of these somber ideas.

JUANA

You are good, Count, and you treat me like a sister as you promised. Oh–why isn't he already here, my dear Luis–to help me discharge my debt to you?

The servants place the candles on the table.

GILBERT

There! Look–great illuminations. These golden reflections escape through the windows and serve as guides to travelers lost in the mountains.

FIRST TRAVELER

At least, if there are ghosts here, we'll see them.

GILBERT

I have little belief in ghosts, even though a Breton, child of the manor of Tiffauges and almost the godson of the fairy Melusina–but I fully believe in thieves, bandits, assassins of the Spanish Sierras, but more than that I believe in audacity, the trickery of these gentlemen. I suspect them capable of having murdered travelers here and not having stolen their purses to spread the rumor in this canton of the presence of supernatural creatures.

FIRST TRAVELER

And to what purpose, Count Gilbert? Tell us that–let's hear it.

GILBERT

For Heaven's sake! With the end of establishing
themselves comfortably in this old castle
Tormenar, which reigns almost inaccessible
above these gorges–with the end of keeping off
police and soldiers who might take it into their
heads to interfere with their operation. But with
us, these gentlemen will lose their trouble. We
are going to keep our weapons about us, place a
guard at the door and another at the window–and
bad luck to whoever tries to frighten us! So be
reassured ladies, you've dried your cloaks over a
good fire, supper is ready, take your place at the
table which doesn't look bad.

JUANA

My God–what if, by some signal, we could
indicate to him we are here?

GILBERT

Oh! That's very easy.
(to a servant)
Give me that trumpet.

He plays a fanfare.

SECOND TRAVELER

Come–to table ladies! To table, gentlemen!

GILBERT

Friends–leave an empty place by the Señora.
You know for whom, dear little sister.

JUANA

Thank you!

GILBERT

You are going to see something, gentlemen. It's one of the chickens of the innkeeper–and it's going to taste better to us here than in his inn.

FIRST TRAVELER

And the wine, too, as it has come a long way.

GILBERT

Gentlemen, we are in the land of Sancho, in the realm of proverbs and, you know, travel educates the young. Señora, I beg you, two drops of wine and a slice of rabbit paté.

JUANA

Impossible! My heart is torn from me. Don't concern yourself any more about my silly person, I beg you. Oh, if you knew how much you dispel sadness with your charming supper.

SECOND TRAVELER

The Señora is sad.

JUANA

No, sir, no.

FIRST TRAVELER

It wouldn't be surprising–the aspect of Tormenar is not exactly joyous.

GILBERT

The fact is, it is neither Versailles nor the
Trianon–but still, there's shelter.

THIRD TRAVELER

Eh–say! It's raining up there.

GILBERT

Truly the chatelain is no good. He ought to
repair the roof.

FIRST TRAVELER

Say, Count, what's it like in your chateau of
Tiffauges?

GILBERT

Larger, but a bit less somber.

SECOND TRAVELER

It seems to me that for a Breton, for a godson of
Melusina, as you said just now–you are indeed
incredulous on the subject of apparitions.

GILBERT

Ah, not so, on the contrary–*peste*! I would not
be from my country. Only, I say that it's a long
while since I saw one.

FIRST TRAVELER

What do you mean a long time?

SECOND TRAVELER

How many years has it been, Count?

GILBERT

Alas, since I've been a man, since I've parted
from those naive and mysterious beliefs of one's
first youth with the help of that cold and sad
light called reason.

THIRD TRAVELER

Then you believe in supernatural creatures, in
ondines, leprechauns, sylphs and fairies?

GILBERT

Why, yes, doubtless. Why assume the chain of
being stops with man?

THIRD TRAVELER

Damn—I believe what I see and what I sense—
I believe in this glass of wine because I hold this
glass and I drink this wine, but I cannot believe
what I don't sense and what I don't see.

GILBERT

And you are wrong, Marquis. There are some
animals you cannot see except with the aid of a
microscope—invented last year, I think—well—for
six thousand years, no one saw these animals for
lack of a microscope—does it follow that, for six
thousand years, these animals didn't exist? If
there are creatures infinitely small, invisible
because of their size, can't creatures exist that
cannot be seen because of their transparency and
whom God, whose messengers they are, allows
to revert to human form to reveal a joy to us or
warn us of a danger? Oh! Marquis, you are not
going to laugh at such enormities? In Brittany,

GILBERT (cont'd)

we don't have a peasant who doesn't possess his
leprechaun who pulls the hair of his horses or
the distaff of his daughter's flax–we don't have
a miller who doesn't have his goblins dancing in
the swamp and on the lakes; not a fisherman
who doesn't have his lady of the water who
foretells for him storms and fine weather; telling
him when he can adventure on the sea or when
he must return to port.

FIRST TRAVELER

And what have you at Chateau Tiffauges,
leprechauns, goblins or lady of the water?

GILBERT

Me? I have an enchanted tapestry.

ALL

What's that?

GILBERT

Oh, it's one of those youthful dreams which I
was telling you about just now–the chatelains of
Tiffauges have the custom of placing their first-
born for a day in what we call in the chateau–the
Tapestry Room. On this Tapestry is represented
the fairy, Melusina, and all her court. Well, is it
a dream as I said just now, or is it a reality?
When I was a child, sleeping my cradle and the
rays of the Moon came through the immense
window, at midnight, I woke up, and then to my
great pleasure, I saw all the personages of the

GILBERT (cont'd)

Tapestry descend. The player of the bagpipes made everyone dance–to silent quadrilles with his silent instrument–whose feet couldn't be heard to resound on the floor–a huntsman chased a stag with his pack all around the room–the birds flew about and came to refresh me with the sight of the beating of their wings–then the fairy herself came to me, all white, all pale, all smiling and she rocked me softly in my cradle, murmuring a song I certainly knew in my childhood–but whose air and words are lost long since in the noise and agitation of this world–all materialist and realistic.

JUANA

Oh! How I believe all that.

FIRST TRAVELER

In fact, each country has its superstition. Look– for example, I took a trip to Epirus. Well, legends change with the character of the inhabitants, with the look of the country. There's no benevolent fairy there, no inoffensive goblins, no joking leprechaun. No, it's the terrible ghoul, evil-doing, murderous, the spectral woman, wearing the appearance of beauty, the forms of youth to better conceal her snares and attacking especially young men, the handsomer, the fresher, the better–whose blood they drink with delight.

JUANA

Horror.

GILBERT

If you were French, Miss, you would know, at
least in translation, of our ingenious compatriot,
Galland–the history of a ghoul who married a
handsome young man, who seeing her eat for
nourishment only some little grains of rice with
little ivory chop sticks, followed her one night to
his great terror–make one of those bloody meals
which the Marquis was just now describing.

JUANA

And have you seen one of those creatures?

FIRST TRAVELER

Well, Señora, I saw a woman who passed for
one.

SECOND TRAVELER

And she was–?

FIRST TRAVELER

A woman like all other women–almost–only,
perhaps a bit taller, a bit poorer, a bit thinner
than ordinary women–with staring eyes, that
shone like an owl's.

GILBERT

Was she beautiful, at least, with all that?

FIRST TRAVELER

Yes, more beautiful than ugly–but a very
singular beauty.

JUANA
Beautiful! Such a monster!

FIRST TRAVELER
Oh, Señora, undeceive yourself–these women
are very coquettish. They don't take by chance
the man for whom they reserve the funereal gift
of infernal love. Those they find unworthy of
them, they let live–but if a man be handsome,
loved by another young and beautiful woman–
they shiver with joy–for at this same time, they
have a man to devour and a rival to drive to
despair. Then, they lie in ambush in some
solitary place. They watch for the passing of
their prey, lull him to sleep with the movement
of their vast wings and, when he is asleep in a
mortal bliss, they aspirate his blood and his life.
They are invisible, they assist in the sorrow of
the fiancée, whose tears they drink with a
voluptuousness equal only to that of drinking his
blood.

JUANA
Señor, Señor–from pity, don't say that.

GILBERT
In fact, we are having a lugubrious conversation
for people who came here with the intention of
having a good time.

JUANA
(taking Gilbert aside)
Señor Gilbert, I beg you, let's go out to meet
Don Luis–just to the outer gate. Let's go. I am

JUANA (cont'd)
dying of uneasiness and fright. I know very well
what you are going to say to me–stories for
children, chimerical dreams! I repeat–I'm afraid
for my fiancé, I'm afraid.

GILBERT
Look, relax, Señora, and believe me. Get rid of
the uneasiness that fills your beautiful eyes with
tears. Certain expected travelers don't arrive
because of the storm which has devastated the
roads. We will see him arrive tomorrow at dawn,
very dry and rosy, freshly breathing the morning
breeze. Don't you find something nice, besides,
in listening to scary stories, near a reassuring
fire, in company of a troop of determined
friends? Outside the storm blows, branches
crack, the birds of the night, frightened, bump
into each other in the air; we, here, savor the
wedding dinner of the innkeeper–we drink the
health of those who are dear to us–and we hold
each other by the hand, we are defying
leprechauns, thieves, ghouls and vampires.

JUANA
Count, I beg you. Let's go out to look for
Don Luis!

GILBERT
Let's do better–this window gives on the ramp
which circuits the castle. Let's go on the balcony
with a torch, call, even, if you like. If Don Luis
is in the neighborhood, he must see us and hear
us.

JUANA

Yes! You are right–come.

FIRST TRAVELER

Are you suffering, Madam?

GILBERT

No, Marquis, but your story has made an impression on the Señora and I will escort her to this window to help her breath some fresh night air.

THIRD TRAVELER

Devil! It seems to me there's no need to go to the window for that.

GILBERT

(calling from the window)

Don Luis! Don Luis!

JUANA

Luis! Luis!

THIRD TRAVELER

The poor child is afraid! Say, Chevalier–what would she have been if you'd told the story of the vampire?

FIRST TRAVELER

What–you've seen a vampire?

SECOND TRAVELER

No, not precisely, but...

THIRD TRAVELER
Oh–don't worry–she's at the window and cannot hear. You ladies are brave like Bradamante and Clorinda.

GILBERT
(calling again)
Don Luis! Don Luis!

FIRST TRAVELER
You didn't see a vampire? But I really want your vampire–I want to marry him to my ghoul.

SECOND TRAVELER
I said I didn't see a vampire–but I was lodging in Peru–in a house inhabited by Jews to whom a vampire paid a visit. These Jews were bankers and very rich–and had several daughters and among them an adorable creature of sixteen. I saw her portrait and really, she was marvelous.

GILBERT
Don Luis! Don Luis!

JUANA
Luis! Oh!

FIRST TRAVELER
Nothing–continue–it's their torch which went out.

JUANA
Ah! My God, I am dying.

ALL

Continue–continue!

Gilbert shuts the window.

SECOND TRAVELER

That night when everyone was asleep in the house, when the lights were dying one by one, then they heard twelve struck on the clock.

THIRD TRAVELER

Heavens, midnight just struck!

GILBERT

Have no fear, Señora, I am here.

SECOND TRAVELER

Then, a noise like the rustle of the wind resounding on the stairway, pale and sinister flames coursed through the corridors and suddenly, at the last tick of the clock–the door opened slowly, and pale, and livid, the vampire appeared–Ah!

Ruthven enters.

ALL

Who are you?

GILBERT

What do you want?

RUTHVEN

Oh, pardon, a thousand pardons, ladies! Excuse me, gentlemen. You ask me who I am–I am a traveler like you, sent away by the innkeeper, Señor Rozo, who is marrying his daughter. They told me that a joyous company had bravely gone up to the Castle Tormenar–and in fact, from down there, I saw the windows which seemed to throw out flames. What do I want–why, since you've found a fine lodging here, I quite simply want you to admit me to your company. I bring my provisions and my arms. I am Lord Ruthven, peer of England, your devoted servant. Put your swords back in their scabbards, gentlemen and you, ladies, pardon me for not having myself announced, but I found no one in the antechamber.

GILBERT

It's for us to ask you pardon, Milord–but your arrival here in the midst of these ruins was so unexpected. Relax, Juana.

RUTHVEN

Oh! But I'm acting frightfully. What, Madam, does my appearance make you so pale and trembling?

JUANA

In truth, Milord, your arrival coincided so strangely with a story they were telling.

RUTHVEN

And what story were they telling?

GILBERT

Why they spoke of–

RUTHVEN

Of what?

THIRD TRAVELER

Of a vampire, Milord.

RUTHVEN

Ah! Ah! Of a–?

SECOND TRAVELER

I was saying that, in Hungary, it's not unusual to hear even more terrible stories told–

RUTHVEN

Yes, surely, but it's much rarer thing to meet the hero of these stories. Me, too, ladies, I've traveled in Hungary and have never seen one.

SECOND TRAVELER

But still, were you never told–?

RUTHVEN

If you please, gentlemen, can't we talk of things more pleasant?

JUANA

Oh! As for me, I beg you.

GILBERT

Milord, permit me to introduce you to those you find yourselves with, the Marquis d'Hecquerey

GILBERT (cont'd)
with his wife and two daughters, the Chevalier
Marini and as for me, Milord, I am Count
Gilbert de Tiffauges. Now, Milord–be welcome.
You said you had some weapons?

RUTHVEN
Here.

GILBERT
Provisions?

RUTHVEN
My valet's bringing it here on a mule.

GILBERT
But I don't see him?

RUTHVEN
Oh, I left him behind arguing with the mule.
He's really very bull-headed a mule and this one
doubtless knows the legend of Castle Tormenar
so well that he resists coming with all his
strength.

GILBERT
But perhaps your servant will get lost?

RUTHVEN
Oh–there's no danger. He's a lad from these
parts that I took from the inn of Master Rozos.
He was looking for a master and I engaged him.
Eh! I hear him! Arrive, lad! Arrive!

Lazare enters.

LAZARE
All the same, here I am! Well, my word of
honor, I didn't know a man could be brave
enough to have such fear of dying.

GILBERT
Why, it's that poltroon of Lazare.

LAZARE
Poltroon! Do you say that to me, here?

GILBERT
What the devil decided you to climb up to
Tormenar?

LAZARE
Listen! I already missed two chances, Madam
and you. Who risks nothing gets nothing.
I swore not to let a third escape. It was this
gentleman who came–he's not the one who
pleased me the most, no, I must say it, but he
was the one who came last.
(looking around him)
You are all still in good condition.

JUANA
My friend.

LAZARE
Ah! It's you, Señora?

JUANA
Yes–you didn't see Don Luis at the inn?

LAZARE
I didn't see Don Luis at the inn, Señora. If
another had come, I assure you, I would have
chosen him.

THIRD TRAVELER
But you aren't eating or drinking, Milord?

RUTHVEN
The cold has taken my appetite.

LAZARE
Why, how funny that is–the cold has such an
effect on him. It has the contrary effect on me.
Good! So I don't have the same character as my
master–Oh–whoever would have told me that I
would be dining at Castle Tormenar!

THIRD TRAVELER
Still, what's wrong with this famous Castle
Tormenar?

FIRST TRAVELER
To me, it seems it's a castle like any other.

LAZARE
Yes, like all the others! He's sweet, this tourist.

SECOND TRAVELER
Absolutely like, a little less dilapidated,
perhaps–that's all.

LAZARE

That's all! Why you don't know what happened
in Castle Tormenar?

GILBERT

Here?

LAZARE

Yes, here, right in this room where we are.

FIRST TRAVELER

Ah! Gentlemen, each of you told us a story–now
this brave lad must tell us his–I bet whatever you
want that it won't be as lugubrious as ours.

LAZARE

Me, tell the story of Castle Tormenar here in
Castle Tormenar even? Come on–never!

FIRST TRAVELER

Why's that?

LAZARE

Why because I already felt myself almost dying
of fear when I told it two leagues from here. And
as for telling it in this castle, I would be afraid of
dying for real!

FIRST TRAVELER

Come on, come here and drink this glass of
wine.

LAZARE

Oh! As to that, I ask nothing better–for the story,
no, no. I don't take a turn like that for myself.
Oh! I don't say if I had two or three glasses of
wine like that in my head.

SECOND TRAVELER

A second, my friend–and to your health!

LAZARE

You do me honor! Ah! No doubt about it, new
wine. Not like Master Rozo's.

FIRST TRAVELER

It is.

LAZARE

It's from Master Rozo's?

THIRD TRAVELER

Be sure of it.

LAZARE

Then I must be mistaken about the bottle.

SECOND TRAVELER

Well–because you've had three glasses of wine.

LAZARE

You think so?

GILBERT

You said there was a Count of Tormenar?

LAZARE

No–Not just one–three.

FIRST TRAVELER

Three!

LAZARE

Yes–there were three Counts of Tormenar. You
see–there was one who was said to have passed
away fifty years ago. Others who say it was a
a thousand years ago, and then others who say
he never died at all.

SECOND TRAVELER

But still, at the present time, there exists no
Count of Tormenar?

LAZARE

Why–what does it matter to you–I ask you?

FIRST TRAVELER

Why–Hell!–When one has been received in
people's home, it's nice to know if you might
meet them someday to thank them.

LAZARE

Ha! You won't meet him–rest assured or if you
meet him, it's some cousin, a collateral who
doesn't bear the family name.

SECOND TRAVELER

Still, to get back to these Counts.

LAZARE

Well, I said each of them had a castle in
Catalonia–one of them, the youngest and most
despicable, invited his two brothers to dine with
him. He's the one who lived in this castle.

THIRD TRAVELER

Ah! The devil!

LAZARE

You really are determined to know the end of
this story?

ALL

Why certainly. By God!

LAZARE

It's that I'd prefer not to tell it.

ALL

The end of the story. The end of the story.

LAZARE

The youngest and most despicable of the three
invited his two brothers to dine–he lit up the
castle as for a feast day, he prepared everything
as if they were going to come.

GILBERT

As if they were going to come?

LAZARE

Yes, but he knew they wouldn't come, the dog,
since he had them murdered on the way.

RUTHVEN

Ah! Ah! Why–do you know your story is
charming, my friend? I'm really pleased to have
taken you into my service; when you have
nothing to do, you'll tell me these stories.

LAZARE

Milord is good. He had them murdered in the
mountains and, as he was naturally their heir,
and since he killed them and their children with
them–he inherited.

THIRD TRAVELER

You forgot the circumstances of the children
which was very important.

LAZARE

I had forgotten, that's right. But that doesn't
matter since I remembered it. He inherited all
three castles.

FIRST TRAVELER

Only two, my friend, since the third was his.

LAZARE

That's right–but then something happened to
him–

THIRD TRAVELER

Which was?

LAZARE

Oh! A bad business completely.

GILBERT

Let's see.

LAZARE

Which was that whenever he sat down to eat, he found one of his brothers was already seated before him–which was–whenever he wanted to go to bed, he found one of his brothers sleeping in the space between the bed and the wall.

RUTHVEN

My dear Lazare, I'm doubling your wages.

LAZARE

I thank Milord much. I know many more stories like that and, if he likes, I can learn others.

RUTHVEN

Ah! This suffices, since you've finished it.

FIRST TRAVELER

But, it is finished, doubtless?

LAZARE

Ah, indeed, yes! The rogue had three children, three boys–handsome and strong–one a student at the University of Salamanca, the second at the University of Valladolid and the third at Coimbra. He made all three come and resolved to go with them to visit his brothers' castles which he did not dare visit alone.

THIRD TRAVELER

That's understandable.

LAZARE

During the first voyage made to one of the
castles, his oldest son died. After the first, he
went to the second and he lost his younger son.
He was obstinate and returned to the first where
he lost his third son.

FIRST TRAVELER

But since he was warned, what the Devil was he
going to do in such a place?

LAZARE

Yes–really–what was he going to in this castle?
It appears that he also said that. So that not
daring to return to the others or his own, he went
to a monastery where he confessed his crime,
did penance and died with the odor of sanctity.
Since that time, the three chateaux have been
deserted and when, by chance, travelers stop to
pass the night, the next morning, one or two are
found dead. That's infallible, that is!

RUTHVEN

In that case, gentlemen, the bad luck will be
mine.

GILBERT

Why's that?

RUTHVEN

Because I was the last to arrive and customarily,
it's on the last that these things fall.

LAZARE

Why no, why no—I was the last to arrive. Wait a
minute! Wait a minute! My God, have I been
stupid enough to tell myself stories that put me
in such fear.

GILBERT

Bravo! Bravo! Lazare! You told marvelously.
Right, gentlemen? Right ladies?

ALL

(laughing)
Marvelously! Marvelously, Lazare!

LAZARE

These gentlemen are very kind, these ladies are
very kind.

GILBERT

Yes, you've forgotten one thing.

LAZARE

You think so?

GILBERT

You've forgotten to tell us about the collateral—
you know—the distant cousin?

LAZARE

Yes—the heir.

GILBERT

Well, why doesn't he inhabit one of the three
castles?

LAZARE

Right! He's careful. He knows you get your
neck broken as soon as you put your foot in
here—and especially members of the family and
since he's a member of the family—

FIRST TRAVELER

He's still living?

LAZARE

Hell, they say so.

THIRD TRAVELER

And do you know his name?

LAZARE

Wait, I know it—he's called, he's called—I've got
it—he's called Don Luis de Figuerroa.

JUANA

Don Luis de Figuerroa! My God! My God!

GILBERT

Wretch!

LAZARE

What's wrong? Ah—you've frightened me—you
have.

JUANA
        (to Gilbert)
Did you hear? Each time an heir of Tormenar
crosses the sill of the castle, he dies.

RUTHVEN

Count, I believe it will be time to find a place
where these ladies can spend the night.

The travelers rise; the servants clear the table.

GILBERT

Lazare!

LAZARE

Señor Count?

GILBERT

There are candles and blankets on the mules,
right?

LAZARE

Yes, Señor Count.

GILBERT

Well, make a distribution, Chevalier! Install
yourself with these gentlemen in the next room.

THIRD TRAVELER

Very well.

GILBERT

Marquis!

FIRST TRAVELER

Oh, don't worry about me, nor these ladies—
we've found and heated a little room.

GILBERT
Marvelous! You, Señora?

JUANA
Me? Sir, I'll spend the night in a chair.

GILBERT
Oh, no–impossible. This room is open to all the
winds.
(going to open a room on the left)
While in there–you'll be as well off as in your
cell in Huesias–you will sleep until morning
which will come in two hours.

JUANA
How somber this room is! One would say an
abyss!

GILBERT
If you like, Doña Juana, I will remain near you.

JUANA
No, no. It's madness. I will take this room,
Count.

RUTHVEN
(bowing)
Señora.

JUANA
(shivering)
Oh.

GILBERT
It's Milord who takes leave of you, Juana.

JUANA
Milord!

GILBERT
(to Ruthven)
Why–where will you lodge?

RUTHVEN
Sir, don't worry about me–I'll look about, I'll
find something.

GILBERT
Well, my friends–we passed the hour of these
fatal adventures–somber midnight has struck
without bringing any other catastrophe, than the
arrival of a new companion–welcome among us.
The thieves seem to be resigned to leaving us in
possession of the castle, the ghouls don't rise.
The vampires are hiding.

RUTHVEN
Goodbye, ladies! Goodnight, gentlemen!

GILBERT
Till tomorrow, my friends, till tomorrow.

ALL
Goodnight–goodbye!

They leave.

GILBERT

Fine, that's that–let's sleep with two ears–but watch with two eyes.

LAZARE

How amusing this is.

GILBERT

Well, lad–aren't you following your master?

RUTHVEN

I forbid him.

Ruthven leaves.

LAZARE

Good thing he forbade me! If he ordered me, I wouldn't have gone.

GILBERT

And why's that?

LAZARE

Heavens! I'm almost accustomed to this room–it's light or almost so. Do you expect me to go hide in these dark corridors full of owls and bats?

GILBERT

Fine, do as you wish. Look, my dear Juana, look my little sister, are you going to relax a little?

JUANA

I'm better.

GILBERT

You know quite well I am here–I'm going to
sleep on this cloak by the chimney–a sigh from
you and I will hear it!

JUANA

Thanks, my loyal friend. Thanks, my generous
brother!

GILBERT

Pray for me tonight, and as I am sure that my
other sister from Tiffauges, Helen, is doing the
same–two angels will have spoken for me
tonight to the Lord. How happy I am!

JUANA

As you deserve. Goodnight, dear brother.

She goes to the window.

GILBERT

Where are you going?

JUANA

The weather is clearing up. The night is
beautiful, the Moon will soon rise.
          (looking outside)
Nothing–no one.

GILBERT

Courage, Juana.

JUANA

Don Luis, my love...

GILBERT

Come on, sister, will you stay with me near the fire? Will that reassure you? Or do you much prefer to spend the night peacefully in this room thinking of Don Luis?

JUANA

Thinking of Don Luis? Yes, you are right, Gilbert. Goodbye, my friend!

GILBERT

Au revoir–don't you mean?

JUANA

Goodbye! If you see Don Luis before me, tell him how much I love him, won't you?

GILBERT

Oh!

JUANA

How much I love him.

She leaves.

GILBERT

Poor child–her spirit is struck. It's true this absence is strange. It seems to me she's weeping.

LAZARE

Yes, sir, I think so–the Señora is weeping a little–that will do her good. Ah–it's like me–if I could only–

GILBERT

Weep.

LAZARE

No, laugh.

GILBERT

Why nothing prevents you–laugh as much as
you wish.

LAZARE
          (trying)
That's so–it's impossible–I think it will be much
easier for me to sleep.

GILBERT

Well–find a place then–here, in this little room.

LAZARE

My word, yes–near you I really like it this way,
for you suit me very well–I don't know why you
reassure me, whereas my master–I don't say
anything ill of him–poor dear man–but he
doesn't inspire me with anything or–yes–he
rather does inspire me with something–he
frightens me. Still, it's stupid to judge people–he
may be the best–you say it's time to go to bed?

GILBERT

Dawn–I think it is the time.

LAZARE

It's true–it's more than the time–I must go to
bed, yes, sir–in this little room.

GILBERT

Have you something against this little room?

LAZARE

No–anyway, I adapt to everything–they said I
was a poltroon outside, yes–perhaps but once
inside–
        (singing)
Never! Never! Never!

GILBERT

Well, will you make up your mind?

LAZARE

Sir–I wish you a good night. A good night, sir.

GILBERT

Thanks! But you will also do well not to wake
me.

LAZARE

Let's go in my little room to sleep! In my pretty
little room to sleep.

He enters. He can be heard uttering a scream.

GILBERT

Imbecile! What the devil are you doing?

LAZARE

        (reappearing, very pale)
Sir! Sir!

GILBERT

What do you want now?

LAZARE

Sir, there's someone in my room.

GILBERT

Go away!

LAZARE

Sir, I assure you–

GILBERT

You were seeing yourself in some mirror, ninny!

LAZARE

In that case, sir, I should have seen myself standing–not someone who doesn't move.

GILBERT

Take this torch.

LAZARE

Sir!

GILBERT

Come on–light me.

LAZARE

Ah, Lord God.

Gilbert goes into the room. Lazare stays on the threshold.

GILBERT

A body!

LAZARE

Ah!

GILBERT

Will you shut up, wretch! Cold. He's really dead. Light, I tell you.

LAZARE

Never! Never!

Gilbert takes the torch and lights the cadaver.

GILBERT

A young man–still smiling–a wound in his throat. How pale he is.

LAZARE

Jesus God!

GILBERT

It's necessary to know who this is–a billfold–a letter–
      (reading)
"*I will be at Tormenar at the same time you are, be cautious, my fiancée, do it for your Juana*"–
Don Luis de Figuerroa, the last of the Tormenar. He came to the rendezvous first. And this poor child who slept there–beside this cadaver? How to tell her the fatal news? I will kill her by telling her.

JUANA
(in her room)

Ah!

GILBERT

I heard a scream. It seems to be her voice.

JUANA

Ah!

GILBERT

Juana, my sister.

Juana appears–hardly able to stand.

JUANA

To me, Gilbert–help–I am dying!

GILBERT

She's dying–murdered.

Gilbert rushes towards Juana's room.

GILBERT

Oh! Ill fortune to whoever–

Ruthven comes out of Juana's room. Gilbert strikes him
with his sword.

RUTHVEN

Ah!

GILBERT

Lord Ruthven–in Juana's room?!

RUTHVEN

Yes–I ran toward the screams of that young girl.
I saw her run out of her room–I followed to help
her, or avenge her–you've run me through–
Count Gilbert–I am dying.

All the torches run in one after the other and press
around Juana.

GILBERT

But the murderer...

RUTHVEN

Fled! Through this open window doubtless.

GILBERT

Oh–Juana. Oh, Milord.

RUTHVEN

Gilbert...

GILBERT

And it's I who killed you! Oh, why? No! We
will save you!

RUTHVEN

All will be useless–I feel sure.

GILBERT

My God!

RUTHVEN

Listen!

GILBERT

Here I am! Here I am!

RUTHVEN

Keep the others away. Time is precious. I must
confide to you my last wishes.

Gilbert gestures the others away.

RUTHVEN

Count, in the religion that I profess, it is the
custom for the dead to be deposed freely on the
Earth and not buried in tombs. Swear to me that,
after my death, you will carry me to a mountain
peak, exposed to the rays of the new Moon–
swear this to me, Count, and I will pardon you
my death, and you will have done for me all you
can do!

GILBERT

I swear it to you! But, while waiting, some help–

RUTHVEN

Useless–death approaches–you swear?

GILBERT

I swear to you!

RUTHVEN

Yourself–the mountain–goodbye!

He dies.

GILBERT

Ah!

LAZARE

(aside)

Lost my situation again!

Blackout.

Scene III

The slope of a hill bristling with naked rocks. Profound night. Vast somber horizon.

Gilbert arrives slowly with the cadaver of Ruthven on his shoulders. He places it on a projecting rock, face turned to the west–then he kneels for a moment beside the body and goes back down the path.

As soon as he disappears, the Moon goes behind some clouds, a bit of its disc shines on the protective rocks and the peaks of the mountains. Light increases and invades the body of the cadaver, little by little, and ends by reaching his face.

Hardly is his face bathed with the light, than the eyes of the cadaver open wide and his mouth smiles lugubriously.

Lord Ruthven first sits up–then rises completely and after having shaken his hair to the wind, he deploys great wings and flies off.

RUTHVEN
You kept your word. Thanks, Gilbert.

CURTAIN.

Act III

Scene IV

At Tiffauges in Brittany–the castle yard.

HELEN

Good news, great news, Jarwick.

JARWICK

Oh, I bet Miss must have received a letter from
Mr. Gilbert.

HELEN

Exactly! So, you understand, Jarwick without
losing a minute.

JARWICK

Yes, everyone must know it! What a feast there
will be in the village, my God. And without
being too curious, when will he arrive, Miss?

HELEN

Today, my friend.

Lahennee enters.

LAHENNEE

Today? Mr. Gilbert is arriving today?

HELEN

Today! This morning! He tells me he will be
here almost as soon as his letter. Oh–dear
brother!

JARWICK

In that case, as you say, there's not an instant to
lose–
　　　　(to the wings)
Hey, boys–Mr. Gilbert is arriving–Mr. Gilbert is
arriving!

He leaves running.

LAHENNEE

Well, Miss, say you are not blessed by the Good
God! You've been waiting for Mr. Gilbert for
six months–you had no news of him–tired of
waiting you were going to marry tomorrow–and
look, he's coming today.

HELEN

Yes, you are right, it was the only thing lacking
to complete my happiness. He's returning and
I am going to be completely happy.

LAHENNEE

Does Miss have orders to give me?

HELEN

What orders do you want me to give you? As
soon as he arrives, I will throw myself into his
arms. As for our worthy peasants. Oh, I am not

HELEN (cont'd)
concerned! From the arrival of my brother, we
are going to see them pour out–we will then run
–Eh! Heavens there they are already–Do you
hear?

LAHENNEE
Aren't you going to tell Baron de Marsden?

HELEN
I am, my friend, and you foresee my wish. Send
someone to tell him my brother is arriving. Let
him come, since tomorrow my brother will be
his brother. I don't need to tell you to choose
your best messenger.

Enter peasants of both sexes, who form a group in the
rear.

LAHENNEE
Oh, don't worry, Miss!

HELEN
Come, my friends.

The peasants come forward.

HELEN
Well, you know? Yes, since you have your
hands full of flowers.

PEASANT GIRL
And flowers from the fields, too. We know you
especially like them.

HELEN

Oh–the charming blues–and what a beautiful
crown I'm going to make for myself of them.

PEASANT GIRL

Damn, Miss–I don't dare offer you these
marguerites and gold buttons. You have such
beautiful flowers in your garden.

HELEN

Give them to me, yes! Give me them. Flowers
that grow in the gardens are the flowers of men–
those which grow in the fields are the flowers of
the Good God.

ALL
(giving her flowers)
Here, Miss, here.

HELEN

Oh! Keep some for my brother.

ALL

Yes–yes–for Milord, we'll scatter them.

HELEN

Oh! He's the true Lord. The lord of our hearts,
right? And he passes above all the others,
except, of course, the Lord God. You know, my
friends, a day of return is a festival day–not only
don't you work but you wear your best clothes
and you dance. Well, soon we'll be dancing
here. Bring all the musicians from the villages–
Lahennee is in charge of refreshments.

A YOUNG GIRL

Ah, Miss!

HELEN

Oh, I know what you want to say, my poor
child–when you return, you'll find a new dress.

A YOUNG GIRL

Oh–may our Lady of Clisson watch over you,
Miss!

HELEN

(to another young girl)
You, Margo, take this gold cross and tell your
fiancé to put it on your neck–you, boy, new
ribbons for your bagpipe, you understand? And
here's a gold medal for your hat.

ALL

What a joy! Long live our good Countess. Long
live our dear Countess. Long live the Countess
of Tiffauges!

HELEN

Yes, children. Thanks! Thanks!

The peasants leave.

HELEN

(alone)
It's good to be loved this way. Each morning
when I come down to the flowerbeds and I see
God smile at me in a ray of sunlight or in the

HELEN (cont'd)

perfume of the meadows, when I notice these
good creations that bow to me like these
flowers–not to render homage to me, thank God,
but to tell me how much they love me, then how
happy I am to think that not all my joy is in that.
I say to myself, I am even richer from the joy
that God promises me than what he gives me.
I tell myself that my brother is going to return,
that I will see him again, that a long stretch of
happy days is reserved for me with this dear
companion of my childhood, and that if I desired
still more–Oh, my God, you have been good
enough to join to this bliss the most precious
love. Oh George! George! You who divine all
my thoughts, you who go before all my desires,
how is it that you haven't divined that my
brother will arrive, and that something will be
missing from my joy if you are not there. When
I embrace him –

(seeing Lahennee enter.)

Well, my friends have you sent to the Baron?

LAHENNEE

I did better: I went myself.

HELEN

Good Lahennee! Well.

LAHENNEE

Well, miss–the Baron isn't at the Chateau.

HELEN

He isn't at the Chateau! And where is he then?

LAHENNEE

Miss, a messenger arrived last night from Nantes
they believe–he demanded they wake the Baron,
who, as soon as he awakened, rose, had his
horse saddled and left.

HELEN

Left! What! Without saying anything to me?

LAHENNEE

In fact, Miss, he ordered that you be informed
that when midday strikes, something will
happen–he will be in the Chateau. I met his
confidential servant who is coming to carry out
his master's commission to you.

HELEN

Ah! That reassures me a bit. Did you tell them to
inform the Baron, as soon as he returns, of the
arrival of my brother?

LAHENNEE

I expressly said so, Miss.

HELEN

And the servant told you when he'll return from
his trip?

LAHENNEE

He said he would be here on the stroke of noon.

HELEN

Well–so be it! Some noise?

LAHENNEE
What's that? I didn't hear anything.

HELEN
Oh, I heard something.
(turning to the Chateau)
Could it be my brother? Let's run, Lahennee.

LAHENNEE
Oh! That's not necessary. I've placed buglers on
the towers–and if it was Mr. Gilbert–you would
be hearing some famous fanfares.

HELEN
What is it then?

Jarwick enters.

JARWICK
Miss! Miss! A messenger who says he just came
from Spain on behalf of Mr. Gilbert.

HELEN
From Spain! On the part of Gilbert! Hasn't
Gilbert come from Spain?

LAHENNEE
From Spain. But I think Mr. Gilbert left Spain
some time ago.

JARWICK
He said Spain, first, and then other countries–but
I no longer remember the names he mentioned.

HELEN

Oh–no matter! No matter! Let him come!

Lazare enters at rear followed by some peasants.

LAZARE

Yes, my friends, from Spain, from Egypt, from
Greece, from Dalmatia, we made a tour of the
world! I've seen the Red Sea, children, I've been
in Jerusalem. Are you Catholics in this country?

ALL

Doubtless, certainly. And good Catholics, too.

LAZARE

Well, I have some water from the Jordan in a
bottle.
        (noticing Helen)
Oh, the beautiful lady!

HELEN

My friend, you are come on the part of Count
Gilbert de Tiffauges?

LAZARE

And you are Miss Helen, right?

HELEN

Yes, my friend–well, where is my brother? What
has happened to him?

LAZARE

Miss, the Count would be here with me if, on this side of Clisson, a little accident had not happened.

HELEN

An accident! To my brother?

LAZARE

No, reassure yourself: To his horse.

HELEN

But my brother? He's all right?

LAZARE

Oh, as for him, he's doing fine. Oh, Miss, it's quite simple, or rather it's not simple at all, sure, at this time, I still don't understand how it could happen–they must shoe horses badly in Brittany.

HELEN

But still, my friend, look, what happened?

LAZARE

Miss, as the Count was in a great hurry to see you and as he left Nantes–the highways are not very passable–at Nantes we took the post, just like at Beirut–only at Beirut it was on camels.

HELEN

And my brother's horse?

LAZARE

Miss, he hadn't gone a quarter of a league from Clisson when it lost four shoes. Can you believe it? Not one, not two, but four! Then as the shoes on my horses had not budged, he said to me: "Run on ahead, and announce my arrival to my sister so she won't be anxious. I will return to Clisson–and in hurrying my horse so he'll have some exercise. I'll be at Tiffauges as soon as you."

HELEN

So, he's coming?

LAZARE

Oh! My God! Yes! In a half-hour–in a quarter of an hour perhaps.

HELEN

So much the better! But you're hot, my friend?

LAZARE

Oh–because I rode hard.

HELEN

And now you are pale.

LAZARE

Pale–you think so?

HELEN

Why yes–and one might even say you are trembling.

LAZARE

Ah! I am trembling? My word, yes! I hadn't
even noticed it–

HELEN

What's causing it?

LAZARE

Oh! I'm going to tell you, Miss, it's that we
Spaniards are very nervous and the least emotion
gets on my nerves.

HELEN

What emotion?

LAZARE

A disagreeable one, Miss.

HELEN

How's that?

LAZARE

Oh, my God, Miss, when you're traveling,
something always happens. Well, for example,
on the way to Constantine, we met a lion–
emotion, you understand. On the banks of the
Nile, I was throwing stones at a kind of tree
trunk which was lying in the Sun; the tree trunk
opened large, gaping jaws. It was a crocodile–
emotion! In Caucasia, we were stopped by
bandits who fired on us–emotion, always
emotion!

HELEN

Oh, my God, something like that has happened to you in our Brittany, my dear friend?

LAZARE

It has! I set my horse at a trot to be here first, according to the Count's order, when arriving a league from the Chateau, maybe less–I saw that I must absolutely pass by way of a road sunk between two hills covered with thickets and woods. This sunken road was very deep–so deep, that I said to myself, "This cannot be a road. I'm afraid of getting lost and I'm going to stop." You'd have done as I didn't, wouldn't you?

JARWICK

No–I would have gone on.

LAZARE

Ah! You would have gone on.

JARWICK

Doubtless, since the Master had said to go on ahead.

LAZARE

Yes, I'm going to tell you, and Miss will understand that. Brittany is not a gay country. These black forests, these red heaths, these greenish lakes, these rocky gorges and then the solitude which is astonishing when you're not accustomed to it. I was a bit astonished. And then I am not unlucky, Madam–I inherited from

LAZARE (cont'd)

my master–from my first, meaning my second.
The first was Old Man Rozo who wouldn't
allow you to puff in the eye of his daughter. The
second was English–he's dead and indeed
unfortunate for him–agreed–but not for me since
I found myself his heir–his natural heir.

HELEN

But, my friend, it seems to me you are mixing
up two stories and if this continues, you will
never finish.

LAZARE

Oh! If it only were two stories, Miss, I'd be out
of it easily–but really it's more than two...
Returning to the sunken road. I have this
devilish gold–when I said gold I mean real gold
which is in my valise. Jingle, jingle–as the
horse trotted. So I said to myself, "If robbers
were to hear it..." Then, I noticed the branches of
a bush which rustled on the hill to the right–and
in the midst of the leaves, I saw–I saw a face
covered with a mask, a frightful mask. "Go on
quickly," shouted the masked man, "or you are
dead." Miss, no one would say I'm easily
frightened. But my horse was–I had trouble
controlling him–he brought me here, you see
much more quickly than at a trot.

HELEN

It's strange what you tell me, my friend. There
are no robbers in this country. But an enemy of

HELEN (cont'd)
Gilbert, perhaps? Ah, Lazare–doesn't this
frighten you? This masked man in ambush on
the road which my brother must follow. Quick!
Quick! My friends, to horse, arm yourselves,
accompany me–let's run to meet him. You will
guide us, my friend. You will show us where
you saw this masked man.

LAZARE
Miss, I ask nothing better than to accompany
you, but would it be possible, just to secure my
valise and my luggage–that is to say of my
defunct master, the peer of England?

HELEN
Oh! How can you think of that when my brother
is in danger?

Trumpets from the towers of Tiffauges.

LAHENNEE
He's here, Miss, he's here!

HELEN
Ah! My God!

The trumpets redouble.

LAHENNEE
Do you hear? Do you hear?

Gilbert enters at the rear.

114

GILBERT

Helen, my dear sister!

HELEN

My beloved brother! Oh, my God, be blessed!

GILBERT

God pardon me, but it seems to me you are
weeping, sis.

HELEN

From worry first of all–and now I weep from
joy.

GILBERT

You were worried? Had you heard? Why, no,
the distance is too great and, you cannot know.

HELEN

We received your messenger.

GILBERT

Lazare, yes–but he cannot know either.

LAZARE

Sir, you must always expect something in the
world.

HELEN

My God–could you have met this masked man?

GILBERT

How did you know?

HELEN

The same Lazare noticed?

LAZARE

Yes–my enemy!

GILBERT

Your enemy, my poor Lazare? I think he had it
in for me more than you.

HELEN

He attacked you?

GILBERT

You are going to see. About a league from here,
you know, in a sunken road cut with rocks and
scrub.

LAZARE

Huh? What did I tell you?

GILBERT

In spite of my impatience, I was obliged to slow
my horse down. Suddenly, I noticed a woman–
one of our Bretons, poor, bent-over, seeming to
ask for alms. I went toward her with some coins
in my hand. I stopped my horse–then, this
woman suddenly dragged me by my cape and
pulled me quickly to her–and I think, God
pardon me, that she embraced me.

HELEN

That's strange.

GILBERT

Yes, but this is stranger still–for, at the moment she pulled me down, I suddenly heard a musket shot and a ball whistle past my ear. If this woman hadn't made that motion, I would be dead.

HELEN

My God!

LAZARE

That's what was waiting for me if my horse hadn't dragged me off. And no woman to kiss me, either.

GILBERT

My first action was to get up and rush towards the woods–but the woman said one sole word, "Flee!" and she struck the croup of my horse with a branch from a bush. My horse bore me off–crossing rocks, thickets, ditches. A second shot was fired, but that one I didn't hear the ball–it was no longer light. To follow me, lightning was needed.

HELEN

And this woman who saved you? What has become of her?

GILBERT

I don't know. I turned back, but she had disappeared.

HELEN

Oh! We will find her, Gilbert, and for this involuntary benefit, we will make her happy and rich until her last day.

GILBERT

Good sister!

HELEN

But I find you pale, fatigued. Have you suffered?

GILBERT

Oh, many things happened on a year's voyage, dear sister.

HELEN

But nothing you did wrong or which displeased you, right?

GILBERT

No, dear Helen, no!

HELEN

Good! Do you want to go in? Are you hungry? Jarwick is waiting for you.

GILBERT

I'm not hungry, thanks. Let me breathe my native air for a while, look at the country sky. Before these silences, the murmuring of the sweet smelling forests and the mild caress of our pale Sun—leave me, dear sister, let me forget and remember.

HELEN

Yes, my brother! Lahennee, my brother will stay here and wants to be alone for a while. This lad you sent me is in your service, Gilbert?

GILBERT

Yes and no. He's attached to me from affection.

LAZARE

Oh, yes–from pure affection–you can really say that.

HELEN

In fact, I believe from what he said, he's rich.

GILBERT

A master he had is dead.

HELEN

Yes, and dead through mischance, he told me.

GILBERT

Yes, by accident, dear sister.

HELEN

Oh, my God! How was that?

GILBERT

Dear sister–

LAZARE

He caught his neck in a gate and he died of it–that's all.

HELEN
What did this man say?

GILBERT
Nothing.

LAZARE
So that his plates, his clothes, his linen and his
money, right, sir, became mine by inheritance
when he fell three-quarters dead in the corner of
this fatal gate. "Alas," he said, "I have no time to
make a will, but there's my valet, Lazare, a
worthy lad, a very honest lad–the peer of
servants and who served me faithfully while he
served me. Well, to this faithful servant, I leave
all that I possess, regretting that I don't possess
more."

Gilbert looks at Lazare pointedly.

LAZARE
I didn't hear very well what he said, but I am
sure he must have said something like that when
the Count held him in his arms.

HELEN
What! He died in your arms, Gilbert?

GILBERT
Yes, sister, yes–but enough on this subject,
Lazare.

LAZARE

The Count told me that, if at the end of six
months, no one claimed it, the inheritance was
mine. It was six months last night. Has anyone
claimed it?

GILBERT

No! Take it and leave me alone.

LAZARE

Oh, sir, how right I am to love you. Now I am
rich, sir–I cease to be your servant, but I will
always be your friend.

HELEN
(to the peasants)
Go, children, go.

LAHENNEE

Pardon, Count, but as Miss said, the return of the
Count ought to be a day of feast and if now the
Count is sad–

GILBERT

No, children, no! I am, on the contrary, happy–
no one could be more happy.

LAHENNEE

Ho, indeed, then everything's going
marvelously! Come, my friends, come. I'll lead
you off but not for long.

He leaves with the peasants.

Helen watches her brother who escorts the peasants out and shakes their hands.

> HELEN
> Oh, how happy I am that George is not here
> now. I much prefer to announce it to Gilbert.

> GILBERT
> Come sit down, dear little sister–guardian angel
> of Tiffauges–you whose prayers made the
> meadows flower and pollinate the crops, you
> who love me.

> HELEN
> How a sister all alone can love!

> GILBERT
> Poor Juana! She was my second sister that entire
> night.

> HELEN
> What's that, Gilbert?

> GILBERT
> Ah? I didn't say anything.

> HELEN
> No, perhaps, but there's a tear in your eye.

> GILBERT
> Don't you know, Helen, that people cry from joy
> as well as sadness? No, don't make a mistake,
> sister. I am the most happy of men–don't I love

GILBERT (cont'd)
everything which makes up joy? Aren't you
happy yourself–and the reflection of your
happiness, doesn't it shine profoundly in my
heart?

HELEN
My happiness yes–you speak the truth, Gilbert–
even before your arrival, I was happy. God led
you to me and my joy is now immense–infinite
like His bounty.

GILBERT
Yes, I understand–you've decided to make this
friend of our childhood, this dear Philip–that my
sweetest hopes have always destined you for.

HELEN
Brother!

GILBERT
In fact, it seems to me that this feast of which all
these good people are speaking, has an odor of
wedding about it.

HELEN
You are not deceived–only–

GILBERT
Only Philip is absent on a trip. Is he going to
return? You are expecting him?

HELEN

Brother, I'm not expecting Philip–Philip isn't in Brittany.

GILBERT

And where is he then?

HELEN

I don't know.

GILBERT

Why did he leave?

HELEN

Because about three months ago, I confessed to him, as a loyal Breton, that I didn't love him.

GILBERT

You didn't love Philip?

HELEN

No, my brother. I mistook the feeling I called love–it was friendship–nothing more.

GILBERT

Well?

HELEN

Well, Philip shook my hand, bowed and passing before me, left. We have not heard anyone speak of him since that day.

GILBERT

Oh, my God! But it's you who are mistaken,
perhaps? Why don't you love Philip, the most
charming, the best of men? Dear sister, you
don't know what love is and, in your ignorance,
you call it friendship.

HELEN

No, brother, no! Today I know the difference
between friendship and love–

GILBERT

You?

HELEN

Yes–someone made me understand by telling
me that he loved me.

GILBERT

Oh, sister–are you really sure?

HELEN

Don't irritate me, Gilbert. Oh, I really struggled!
I even tried to withdraw from this all-powerful
influence which, for five months, has dominated
and absorbed me entirely. Oh, if you knew the
efforts I made to love Philip! But my heart no
longer belongs to me, my will is another's, my
words change their meaning in crossing my lips–
even my thoughts betray. I invoke to myself the
image of Philip and another image appears–
triumphant and exclusive–what can I say to you,
Gilbert? My days and my nights are passed and

HELEN (cont'd)
consumed in a singular contemplation–
everything around me has disappeared, smashed,
melted, effaced, by this devouring passion!
Now, listen and judge! I, who cried so much
over your absence–I never cried any more in
thinking of you–I, who had spent so many days
watching the road from Nantes by which you
would return–I spend my life watching turrets of
the chateau where George lives. That's when
I wrote you to return right away, without losing
a minute, for I no longer understand myself–
I feel myself becoming mad–without the power
to hold myself back from the slope of dizzy
madness. I wrote to you to return. I set a time for
you, tomorrow! For, if you hadn't returned
before tomorrow, you would find me married,
married, my dear brother, without having had
your hand to escort me to the altar–and now,
look, brother, see if ever I was able to love
Philip so! Tell me, if this is indeed what they
call love!

GILBERT
You overwhelm me! And you are loved, at least.

HELEN
I think so!

GILBERT
And he who loves you?

HELEN

Oh–don't worry about anything Gilbert–worthy
of me, worthy of us! He's a fine gentleman, rich
and honored.

GILBERT

From this country?

HELEN

No, but for five months, he's been established
here.

GILBERT

His name?

HELEN

The Baron George Marsden–I believe he's of
Scot descent.

GILBERT

Young?

HELEN

It's difficult for me to tell his age. I think he's
thirty or thirty-five.

GILBERT

And of his person–how is he?

HELEN

Oh–you understand I find him handsome.

GILBERT

Baron Marsden.

HELEN

Oh, don't be biased against him—I know you've got it in for him, down deep for having driven your childhood friend, poor Philip, out of my heart. Alas, it's not his fault nor mine. You won't reject this sweet belief in the sympathy and meeting of souls? Be generous then, Gilbert, and don't look with rage at the one you should call your brother. And if you find his face a little pale and somber, pity him, for he's sad, he says, and he only suffers from an excess of love for me.

GILBERT

And does Helen promise to love in her turn the one she must call her sister?

HELEN

What do you mean, brother?

GILBERT

Listen! I pardon you much more easily since I myself have need of pardon—I've committed the same crime as you.

HELEN

You love?

GILBERT

Yes.

HELEN

Ah—what's she like? Tell me, young, blonde, brunette, charming?

GILBERT

Seventeen, blonde, charming, yes.

HELEN

And the name?

GILBERT

Antonia.

HELEN

Is she Italian, Spanish?

GILBERT

Dalmatian. I was traveling the road from Almira
to Spalatro when we were attacked by bandits.
Wounded while I defended myself from them,
I was taken to a neighboring villa. That's where
Antonia and her mother lived. Antonia, more
beautiful than you can imagine, under her
mourning.

HELEN

Mourning?

GILBERT

Yes, for she had just lost her father. If not, you
should have seen me with her. Dear Helen,
you'd have seen me married. I would have
waited until the end of her mourning with her,
that is to say in a paradise that lacked only you,
Helen, when I got your letter that told me to
return without losing a minute.

HELEN

You returned!

GILBERT

See if I love you! For you, I left Antonia, but I promised to return. In six months, her mourning will be over and Antonia can become my wife!

HELEN

Well–we shall all go to Spalatro! I will replace Antonia's black veils with a white wedding dress. Oh, he's a great traveler, Baron Marsden! Like you, he has been to Spain, Egypt and Syria. I think, dear Gilbert, that it was one of his seductions to be able to speak to me of places where you were.

GILBERT

And when can I see him, this so-well cherished Baron Marsden?

HELEN

At noon. Why, would you like me to send for him?

GILBERT

Oh, noon will be soon here. You know, I have no need of a watch here–I know where the Sun marks the time at each step it takes. You see, at the moment, it is lighting the roof of the chapel. When it has reached the extremity of the bell turret, it will be noon. And then, look at our

GILBERT (cont'd)

peasants, lads and lasses–who come in great
pomp with fiddlers in the lead. Wait here, Helen,
and be satisfied with yourself, for having alone
and by your side, a brother who left everything
to return to you.

HELEN

Oh, conceited brother!

Lazare enters, followed by some peasants.

LAZARE

Mr. Gilbert.

GILBERT

Ah–it's you, Lazare.

LAZARE

Count, tell me, I beg you, while these peasants
are going to dance, can't you lend me some
penman who can write me an inventory of all
my inheritance and draw up a contract for an
acquisition I want to make?

GILBERT

An acquisition?

LAZARE

Yes–

GILBERT

In Brittany?

LAZARE

Decidedly the country please me. I am disgusted with Spain—you know why, don't you? Here, the women are pretty, the houses have doors and windows. I want to buy myself a house and a woman.

GILBERT

That's fine. Go find my intendant Lahennee—he will do what you ask—but if you wish to please me, Lazare don't speak to me of Spain or your inheritance.

LAZARE

Ah, yes, I understand. Wait—it's that little house down there in the Sun—and that big girl who's in the shadows.

Exit Lazare.

A SERVANT
(announcing)
Baron Marsden.

HELEN

Here he is! Be good to him, Gilbert!

GILBERT
Oh, don't worry, sis.

"Marsden" (Ruthven) enters. He and Gilbert walk towards each other—at first, the peasants are preventing them from seeing each other. But they suddenly stand aside and the two find themselves face-to-face.

GILBERT

My God!

HELEN

What's the matter?

GILBERT
          (aside)
It's him!

RUTHVEN

Good day, Count.

HELEN

Gilbert!

GILBERT

You are Baron Marsden?

RUTHVEN

And your most devoted servant, Count.

HELEN

What's wrong with Gilbert, George?

RUTHVEN

The memory of an adventure that passed
between us, perhaps.

HELEN

You know my brother, then?

RUTHVEN

Yes.

HELEN
You knew Baron Marsden, brother?

GILBERT
Helen, Helen, get everyone away from here and allow me to speak briefly with this gentleman.

HELEN
You know what you promised me, Gilbert.

GILBERT
Yes, don't worry!

Everyone moves away from Gilbert and Ruthven, who stand alone in the foreground.

GILBERT
You will excuse me, Milord, for you understand my astonishment, don't you?

RUTHVEN
Yes, surely–I am the last person you expected to see again.

GILBERT
Living! Living!

RUTHVEN
Doubtless! Do you regret it, Count?

GILBERT
You, whom I saw fall covered with blood–you, whom I held dying in my arms–you, whom I left dead on the rocks! Impossible! Impossible!

RUTHVEN

What's that? Is it the first time a wound was
taken for mortal that later proved not to be? And
haven't you ever seen a faint simulate death?
Well, I was wounded, I fainted, the fresh
morning air revived me from my lethargy–
I rose, I called–no one! At the first houses where
I knocked to ask for help, they told me you had
left precipitously in great haste. Where to find
you? To go by luck is dicey, the world is large!
I commenced to get well, and as I was sure of
finding you at home in Brittany, when you
returned, as I had to thank you for having
followed my instructions, and consequently, for
having saved my life–for, without you, they
would brutally have buried me in the earth and
as my good genius doubtless pointed the way
here also, I came to Tiffauges. I bought some
land in the neighborhood, and I waited. In the
meantime, joy, I am much too thankful to
providence to say "chance"–in the meantime,
I say, happiness made me meet your sister–
I loved her and I succeeded in inspiring some
esteem in her–I came to say to you today: Count
Gilbert, are you annoyed that I live? My brother,
do you refuse to extend your hand to me
fraternally?

GILBERT

Milord, you were called Lord Ruthven when
I knew you in Tormenar–why have you changed
your name?

RUTHVEN

It's the name of the younger men in our family–
my older brother, Lord Marsden, died, and left
me the heritage of his name and fortune.

GILBERT

You are right–nothing more natural. Excuse me,
Milord, I feel that all my questions are fatiguing
for you–but–

RUTHVEN

Oh–finish–get it over!

GILBERT

Why did you hide from Helen the fact we knew
each other?

RUTHVEN

First of all, Count, our acquaintance was short;
then, as brief as it had been, you had committed
some wrongs toward me–that of killing me, for
example. I wasn't sure what you wished to tell
and what you wished to keep to yourself in all
this story–and, in doubt, I followed the precept
of the wise and I abstained.

GILBERT

Strange! Strange!

HELEN

(coming forward)
Well, brother?

RUTHVEN

Well, Miss, the Count, who first recognized me
only a little, has finally recognized me, and he
permits me to avail myself of the title of his
friend.

GILBERT

Ah.

HELEN

Are you sick? Are you tired, Gilbert?

GILBERT

Yes.

HELEN
(to a servant)
The Count's chamber.

SERVANT

It's ready, Miss.

GILBERT

Oh! I'm choking!

Ziska enters, dressed in a peasant costume.

ZISKA
(low to Gilbert)
Sleep tonight in the chamber of the Tapestry.

GILBERT
(aside)
The beggar woman to whom I owe my life.

ZISKA

Hush!

RUTHVEN
(aside)
A woman spoke to him.

HELEN
Are you coming brother? Au revoir, George!

RUTHVEN
Get a good sleep, Count.

GILBERT
(aside)
In the chamber of the Tapestry–fine! I'll spend the night there.

Exit Helen and Gilbert.

Ruthven watches as Ziska disappears.

RUTHVEN
Disappeared!

Lazare re-enters.

LAZARE
(to himself)
This is fine, this is my account. A work box all in vermilion and gold–worth nearly three thousand francs–three thousand pounds in money and jewels, and thirty thousand pounds in money and bills on the Bank of England–

LAZARE (cont'd)
in all thirty-six or thirty-seven thousand pounds.
Nice little sum, my word! Word of honor!
I would give ten hours to see the deceased face-
to-face and say to him, "I thank you, shade of
Lord Ruthven."

RUTHVEN
(turning)
Huh?

LAZARE
(awestruck)
Ah!

RUTHVEN
Ah! Is it you, Lazare? Tonight we are sleeping
in the Castle Tiffauges, my friend. Carry my box
and my trunks to my room.

LAZARE
Ooo!

RUTHVEN
And give me my purse, so that, tomorrow, I can
pay your comrades for my welcome at Castle
Tiffauges.

LAZARE
Mercy.

RUTHVEN
(aside)
I intend to know who this woman is and what she said.

LAZARE
I am ruined.

Blackout.

Scene V

At the Castle Tiffauges, a huge room hung with a life-
size tapestry of the Fairy Melusina with a Shepherd
playing bagpipes, a Huntsman, a bird on his fist, Sylphs
and Ondines, in pleasant scenery. In the midst of a panel
at the rear is a large frame on which is painted one of the
old Barons de Tiffauges leaning on two knights.

Gilbert is asleep in an armchair. The Fairy Melusina de-
taches from the tapestry and slowly approaches him.

MELUSINA
He's sleeping, and like him, so is half the Earth.
Those who live by day and sleep by night.
Shut their weary eyes, while with mystery
The other half noiselessly awakes.

For of the two mighty Kings you support, O
[world,
One is named Day, the other Darkness
Fertile Darkness is the Mother of Dreams
Sterile Day is the King of Reality.

She turns towards the enchanted Tapestry and addresses
the persons represented.

MELUSINA
Day is dethroned; we reign for twelve hours
The world of the night, my brothers, is ours!
Sleeping mortals deliver their dwellings to us,

MELUSINA (cont'd)
Wake up, brothers, wake up!

One by one, the figures escape from the Tapestry and disappear.

MELUSINA (cont'd)
Shepherd, awake! Day, under the bower,
Had extinguished the joyful sounds of your
[pipes.
But in darkness, your rural jig
Awakens to dance on silent feet.

Huntsman, awaken, who on your gloved hand
Wear the white falcon, fierce nursling of the
[North.
And the screech owl exhales bloodily into the
[woods,
Its last scream under the beak that gnaws it.

Imprisoned sylphs embalmed in roses,
Ondines enveloped in the mist of waters,
Salamanders, rolling in the fumy waves
Mysterious wills-o'-the-wisp sliding on their
[reeds

From the tapestry hasten to descend
The heather shivers and the reed complains
Beneath its ashes the poorest hearth keeps
[preserved
From yesterday's fire, an ill-extinguished spark.

There you are my cherished sister;
Go join our other sisters,

MELUSINA (cont'd)

Who, down there, on the prairie
Do a round dance atop the flowers.

Ondine with blonde tresses
With coral bracelets,
Go seek in the ocean's depth
Your beautiful crystal palace.

Across the watery veil
Extended before your eyes
You'll see the star shine
That gold coin in the skies.

Greetings, scarlet salamander!
Have you then no care
Of the fire that lurks beneath the ashes
In the back of the darkened hearth?

Sister, depart, and on its wing
Let the breeze carry you.
And under your breath
Let the last spark be reborn.

You'll reignite the flame
In the dismayed hearth
As God reignites a soul
In a lifeless body.

To your sports, companions! The gate is open.
Sylphs, they are awaiting you on the green heath
Ondines, plunge into the blue lake waters
Salamanders, play in the folds of fire.

MELUSINA (cont'd)
Alas! For this sad and plaintive night
Far from you, my friends I will remain captive.
But my absence will not trouble you in any
                              [degree.
Earth, water, fire are awaiting you, go!

The figures emerge from the Tapestry and vanish into
the thickness of murals. Melusina comes close to
Gilbert.

MELUSINA
Gilbert, do you recall the happy time
When, with her nursling
Melusina rocked the harmonious cradle
With a song?

That song, Gilbert, was always the same
But it pleased the child
To hear the mouth it loved murmur
An eternal couplet.

You knew, Gilbert, but you've forgotten
The song of yesteryear
So a horn forgets the drowned fanfare
In the fog of the forest.

Indeed, since these notes were spread forth
Twenty years have passed
For 20 years, Gilbert, oh! How many wasted
                              [hours
Life has stolen!

In this very room, child, where your sweet nap

Heard me murmur
MELUSINA (cont'd)
You return today, no longer child but man
And return to weep.

But fear not, my son! I am watching over the
[flame
Of your green spring.
Listen, listen, carefully to what the soul is going
[to tell you
Speaking to your sleep.

Melusina goes to the portraits of the Barons de Tiffauges.

MELUSINA
Now, High Barons of Castellany
Knights without reproach, ancestors of Gilbert.
Under velvet folds or steely mail
Live until the hour of night is ended!

Come, we are alone, I call on you, you!
It is forbidden to reveal to men;
The terrifying secrets of the world we live in,
But God allows us to speak of them amongst
[ourselves.

Come! Over this child, the hope of your race,
On Helen, his sister, hangs a dark danger.
Of misfortunes that this place brings to strangers
Our voices shall avert like a passing dream

And the Angel of the Night, silent watcher,
Who shuts weary eyes with his finger

MELUSINA (cont'd)
Will allow our vows and our thoughts to
[penetrate
The mind of Gilbert whose eyes, he has closed.

The scene comes to life. The Old Baron comes forward
with the two Knights.

OLD BARON
Yes, misfortune is descending on the ancient
[dungeon,
Thanks, for warning us!
Awakened dust at your prophetic voice
We are here! We are here!

MELUSINA
Know that this man with the somber face
What a plot he weaves.
This man, who like us, is a child of shadow
But a cursed child.

Even to our glance his night is too dark
For what strange plan
Does the Lord allow him to live in this world,
Immortal assassin?

No one knows him; God put the whitest doves
In his fatal hands;
And his track can be found near tombs
That he engenders on his path.

Gilbert turns in his sleep feverishly, and begins moaning.

MELUSINA

No virgin escapes the murders that he amasses;
The hideous oppressor
Braves the elements and commands space.

GILBERT

O my sister! O my sister!

MELUSINA

Hardly had his victim Juana expired.
The ghostly ravisher
Stealing from the tomb, returns to the hunt.

GILBERT

O my sister! O my sister!

MELUSINA

Yesterday, he wanted to kill our son in the plain;
For the bloody fiancé
Was counting on depriving Helen of her
                                        [defender.

GILBERT

O my sister! O my sister!

MELUSINA

Let's pray that Almighty God will inspire
                                [Gilbert
To a generous effort.
Ruthven is a demon, Ruthven is a vampire
His love is death.

Now, High Barons of Castellany
Knights without reproach, ancestors of Gilbert

147

MELUSINA (cont'd)
You have heard me and my task is ended.
Sleep, under velvet or in steely armor
You kept your word. Thanks, Gilbert.

As for us, before long dawn will reappear.
Quick, sylphs, ondines, salamanders, wills-o'-
[the-wisp
Huntsman with the white falcon, shepherd who
[beneath the beeches
Leads fantastic dances–

Run, resume your accustomed place
If not, dawn outside, will surprise you in
[confusion
You know at night, O beloved troupe
That when day is, you are no more.

The Sun is going to climb under the azure vault
Let's leave to the King of Day, the burning
[empire of the skies
And let us all become, in this lighted chamber
Motionless and silent.

CURTAIN.

148

Act IV

Scene VI

A terrace on the Chateau Tiffauges. Night.

LAZARE
(alone)

Huh? What? No one! What an idea he had to
give me a rendezvous at three in the morning!
A master who doesn't sleep–who doesn't eat,
who doesn't laugh and when he seems dead,
returns and who is not ashamed to make a poor
devil of servant give back all his inheritance, for
it would be useless for Mr. Gilbert to say that he
made a will in my favor when he was
whispering to him in the ruins of Tormenar–and
now that he has returned, what am I busy with,
I ask you? Instead of saying to me, "Lazare, my
good Lazare, my dear Lazare, I see that the joy
you have in seeing me again breaks your arms
and legs, go to bed my good friend–repose–
sleep!" No, he makes me run from house to
house after an old woman whose name he won't
tell me, whose address he won't give me, whose
description he cannot give me–Oh, Spain, Oh,
Master Rozo, Oh, Petra, when I think that I am
reduced to missing all that, even the ruins of
Tormenar–

Ruthven enters. Lazare shivers.

LAZARE

Milord?

RUTHVEN

Eh–do I frighten you?

LAZARE

Oh–for goodness sake! On the contrary,
Milord!

RUTHVEN

I saw you shivering.

LAZARE

It's because I didn't expect you, Excellency.

RUTHVEN

Fine! I gave you a rendezvous here.

LAZARE

True, I must say it's true. I wouldn't be here if
you hadn't given me a rendezvous.

RUTHVEN

Well, did you find the woman I indicated to
you?

LAZARE

I visited, one after another, all the houses in
Tiffauges–there are eighty. In those houses,
there are ninety-seven women, of which thirty-
nine are old. I talked to all, except for five, of
which three were idiots and two are paralytics.
Not one spoke yesterday to Count Gilbert.

RUTHVEN

My dear, Lazare, you are a lad full of
intelligence.

LAZARE

Am I, Milord?

RUTHVEN

And who serves me faithfully.

LAZARE

Oh, as to that, yes.

RUTHVEN

Which is even more fine on your part, since
I think that my return upset you at first.

LAZARE

Oh! Milord thinks that–

RUTHVEN

Damn, it's quite simple–you thought I was dead,
my poor Lazare, and in that belief, you became
my universal heir.

LAZARE

Milord, it's that–

RUTHVEN

You did the right thing.

LAZARE

Ah, Milord confesses that, when whispering to
Mr. Gilbert, he was–?

RUTHVEN

Yes, my friend, it was to leave you my fortune.

LAZARE

I was sure of it.

RUTHVEN

Also, my dear Lazare, I intend that my return, rather than injure your interests, be profitable to you.

LAZARE

Really?

RUTHVEN

Good servants are rare and one doesn't know how to do too much for them. You are a good servant, Lazare, and I intend to enrich you in my service.

LAZARE

Oh! Yes, that's a fine idea you've got there.

RUTHVEN

You find it so?

LAZARE

I find it so, yes, sir–and I will add–the sooner the better.

RUTHVEN

Well, to that end, we are going to make a bargain, Lazare.

LAZARE
Willingly, sir, if it's good for me.

RUTHVEN
Excellent!

LAZARE
Let's see the bargain.

RUTHVEN
Each time that I put a question to you before someone and that you affirm, each time I question your memory and you are of my opinion, eveb if it's a frivolous matter, I will give you a guinea–if it's an important matter, I will give you ten.

LAZARE
Oh, sir, you are always right and as you are a serious man, it will always be for grave motives.

RUTHVEN
So, you accept?

LAZARE
At once, sir!

RUTHVEN
Then you are of my opinion about it?

LAZARE
Yes, completely!

RUTHVEN

Well, I shall begin to put it in action, here's a guinea.

LAZARE

I think that Milord doesn't attach as much importance to our bargain as it deserves.

RUTHVEN

You are right–and here's ten guineas.

LAZARE

(pocketing the money)

Thanks, sir.

RUTHVEN

So then–it's a treaty concluded.

LAZARE

Treaty concluded.

RUTHVEN

But also every time you are not of my opinion–

LAZARE

But since I always will be–

RUTHVEN

Lazare, there's such as thing as conscience.

LAZARE

You think so?

RUTHVEN

Each time you are not of my opinion–depending
on the importance of the discussion–you will
give me one or ten guineas.

LAZARE

Why, say–sir–

RUTHVEN

You hesitate?

LAZARE

But, but, but–

RUTHVEN

Fine! You don't share my opinion, you are free,
but–
          (extending his hand)
You know–

LAZARE

Sir, what do you mean? I don't share your
opinion? On the contrary, I am completely of
your opinion–twice as much as you are.

RUTHVEN

Then it's agreed?

LAZARE

Heavens!

RUTHVEN

Countess Helen! Leave me.

LAZARE

Instantly, sir, instantly.
(aside)
Decidedly, I was prejudiced against Milord–he
must be good.

Lazare leaves.

RUTHVEN

If this woman who spoke to Gilbert was a
human being, a natural creature, I should have
found her since last night.

Helen enters.

RUTHVEN

You–Helen–what unhoped-for happiness.

HELEN

How long have you been here, George?

RUTHVEN

Why perhaps a quarter of an hour.

HELEN

Well–it's a strange thing–hardly did you get here
when, in the midst of my sleep, I desired your
presence–and woke up. I am tempted to think
sometimes that you have something superhuman
about you and that the love you've inspired in
me is something magical and marvelous.

RUTHVEN

Then what shall I say, my beautiful Helen, since
I awake every day at dawn, not, alas, to your
approach, but to your memory.

HELEN

So that last night–?

RUTHVEN

Oh! Last night–I did better than wake up–I never
slept.

HELEN

And why's that?

RUTHVEN

Do I know myself? Agitated, feverish. I haven't
the courage to return home.

HELEN

How's that?

RUTHVEN

No, I spent the night in the park–the breeze
refreshed me–I heard it come by and flee
through the trees. I hurled your name at it–and it
seemed to me that in parting from me it
repeated–Helen! Helen! Oh! Swear to me
nothing can ever separate us any more.

HELEN

And what do you think can separate us?

RUTHVEN

How do I know? You know, Helen, the closer
happiness approaches, the more one doubts.
Fantastic and capricious demon–when you
extend your hand to seize it, it escapes us.
Helen–comfort me–I doubt–Helen–reassure me,
I'm afraid.

HELEN

My brother, right? Gilbert?

RUTHVEN

Tell me again that my fears have no
foundation–did you see the way he greeted me?

HELEN

Oh! George, you mustn't be angry with him–
although he has always left me the freedom of
my heart, Philip was his childhood companion
and he loved him tenderly. It was Philip that he
wanted to put joy in my life. Give him time to
know you, George, and he will love you as he
loved Philip.

RUTHVEN
        (smiling)
I doubt it.

HELEN

Why doesn't he like you? Look–didn't you have
a frank explanation with him?

RUTHVEN

Oh, on the contrary, very frank.

HELEN

Well?

RUTHVEN

Love or hate doesn't always depend on us.

HELEN

Gilbert is tender and generous–it's not difficult
to inspire his affection.

RUTHVEN

Yes, his character easily receives influences,
vivid impressions. Wait, yesterday–didn't you
notice something? After the first astonishment
caused by my presence–he returned to me, we
shook hands–well, suddenly, his tone, his
language changed–he separated from me–he
kept me at a distance, with such coldness that
I didn't know what more to say to him. Someone
said a word to him, one word and that word
sufficed.

HELEN

What?

RUTHVEN

You didn't notice that woman?

HELEN

A woman?

RUTHVEN

Yes, who seemed aged–and wore the costume of
one of your Bretons.

HELEN

No, I didn't remember–but wait, she was the woman who saved his life before, doubtless?

RUTHVEN

Who saved his life?

HELEN

Yes, yesterday.

RUTHVEN

Yesterday?

HELEN

Oh–right, you didn't know–Gilbert was almost assassinated yesterday–a man ambushed him on a sunken road and fired two rifle shots at him and, but for this woman who grabbed him by his cloak to kiss him, he was a dead man! This woman–he saw her here again yesterday–and she's the one you saw. Well, George, what bad influence can come from her? What advice can this old Breton woman have given Gilbert against you? You don't reply? Why that doubting smile on your lips?

RUTHVEN

They wanted to assassinate your brother, Helen?

HELEN

It's strange isn't it?

RUTHVEN

Yes, truly, so strange that–

HELEN

You doubt it?

RUTHVEN

Wait, Helen–don't ask me–that would be better.

HELEN

Why no, on the contrary, speak.

RUTHVEN

In that case, dear and beautiful Helen, let's
reason–look, tell me, who in this country could
have an interest in the death of your brother?

HELEN

No one.

RUTHVEN

Do you know of any enemy he has?

HELEN

None!

RUTHVEN

Well, then, if no one has any interest in his
death–if you know of no enemy–do you
seriously believe in this attempted assassination?

HELEN

Gilbert said so.

RUTHVEN

Oh!

HELEN

And then Lazare noticed the assassin.

RUTHVEN

Lazare?

HELEN

Yes–a masked man armed with a rifle.

RUTHVEN

Oh! First of all, dear Helen, never cite Lazare to
me as an authority. Lazare is a poltroon, afraid
of his own shadow–moreover he's Spanish–in
other words, superstitious and fanciful.

HELEN

What! George, you think my brother would have
made this up?

RUTHVEN

Made it up–not at all. He's of good faith–and
doubtless he believes he saw it.

HELEN

What do you mean, he believes?

RUTHVEN

Dear Countess, have you carefully observed
your brother since his arrival?

HELEN

Doubtless.

RUTHVEN

Have you listened with attention to all his words?

HELEN

Certainly!

RUTHVEN

Have you compared him to what he was in the past?

HELEN

Why do that?

RUTHVEN

Ah–because it seems to me you should have noticed–

HELEN

What?

RUTHVEN

That you ought to have remarked –

HELEN

Get to the point!

RUTHVEN

Something unusual about him.

HELEN

Oh, my God!

RUTHVEN

Oh–don't get so uneasy–doubtless, since you,
his sister, you, who love him, you, that he
adores– since you notice nothing, his illness is
not as great as I was told. So much that I, aside
from this story of assassination–I found his
conduct not only quite natural but even
reasonable–so he must be better–much better.

HELEN

Better! Why, what do you mean?

RUTHVEN

I mean, dear Helen–pardon me for being the
messenger of such bad news. I mean your
brother was mad!

HELEN

Mad! Gilbert!

RUTHVEN

Yes, but he's been cured. You see, as you didn't
notice it–although I am obliged to tell you.

HELEN

Oh! George–to what cause do you attribute this
madness?

RUTHVEN

A terrible accident.

HELEN

What?

RUTHVEN

Gilbert thought he killed one of his friends.

HELEN

Oh–my God–how can that be? A duel?

RUTHVEN

No–by mistake, without intending to.

HELEN

Tell me then, George. But no, you are mistaken.
It's impossible.

RUTHVEN

This friend–it was me, Helen.

HELEN

Oh, what are you telling me!

RUTHVEN

The truth–pure and simple. We were in Spain in
an old deserted castle where the storm had
driven us, him, me, some travelers, to find a
shelter. We were sleeping when the shouts of a
young Spanish woman named Juana woke us.
Some bandits had got into the castle. I wanted to
help the young woman. Count Gilbert drew his
sword in the shadows and ran me through the
breast. I fainted. Since that time, your brother
has been pursued by the idea that he assassinated
a man and his mind is affected. Since that night,
the world is full of ghosts, spectres, supernatural
beings–that's what caused me yesterday to fear

RUTHVEN (cont'd)
seeing your brother. That's what made me so
wretched in his presence, that's what made him
so embarrassed around me.

HELEN
Oh–my beloved brother.

RUTHVEN
Do you understand, now, Helen, this sick spirit?
Your marriage with me can displease him–and
then I am lost.

HELEN
What do you mean, lost?

RUTHVEN
Doubtless, if he's going to oppose our union–
dear Helen–will you have the courage to resist
your brother?

HELEN
You know how faithfully I love, George, and
that my word is sacred. Here's my hand! Well,
this promise is not enough for you?

RUTHVEN
Helen, you know everything was agreed for
today–it seems to me that any delay will be
deadly to my happiness.

HELEN
And why should we change something which
has been decided, George?

RUTHVEN

Your brother can demand a delay.

HELEN

Why suppose that?

RUTHVEN

My God–who can answer for a sick man?

HELEN

Listen, George–I want to reassure you right
away–you yourself chose the hour of the day
you will become my spouse

RUTHVEN

Oh, instantly, instantly, I will run to the
Chaplain's home–thanks, thanks, dear Helen.
See you again in a few minutes!
    (aside)
Oh, let him come, let him speak now, no matter.
Helen will never believe him.

He leaves.

HELEN

    (alone)
Oh, my God, what he's said to me and what
terrible secret has been revealed to me! Gilbert!
Poor Gilbert! Really, yesterday, on his arrival,
he was sad, pale, almost distracted and seeing
George, he seemed struck down. Oh, Gilbert, be
tranquil. I will be so good, so patient, so
attentive that, even as George's breast cured its
wound, your poor troubled spirit will cure its.

Lahennee enters, running.

> HELEN
>
> But what's wrong? They are running! Lahennee, my God what is it now?

> LAHENNEE
>
> Miss! Miss! Ah! You are there.

> HELEN
>
> What do you want?

> LAHENNEE
>
> My God, what has happened to the Count?

> HELEN
>
> What's this?

> LAHENNEE
>
> Yesterday evening, he ordered me to wake him in the morning, consequently ten minutes ago I went into his room.

> HELEN
>
> Well?

> LAHENNEE
>
> He hasn't slept–his bed is not disturbed.

> HELEN
>
> My God!

LAHENNEE

I soon came away, calling him, asking everyone
for him, when suddenly, I saw him leave the
tapestry room–pale, eyes haggard–calling you–
and–hold, hold, there he is!

HELEN

Gilbert! It's true, Gilbert! My Gilbert!

Gilbert enters, gesticulating wildly.

GILBERT

Helen! Helen! Ah–there you are! God be
praised! Leave us, Lahennee.

He falls into a chair. Lahennee leaves.

GILBERT

Baron George, Lord Marsden, where is he?

HELEN

You want to speak to him?

GILBERT

Yes, instantly, it's necessary I see him.

HELEN

It's necessary?

GILBERT

Yes!

HELEN

He was here just a moment ago.

GILBERT

Oh–the wretch!

HELEN

Gilbert!

GILBERT

Where is that man?

HELEN

He must be in the chapel.

GILBERT

In the chapel? You are mistaken, it is impossible
that the man would dare pray to God.

HELEN

He went to the chapel, not to pray to God, my
friend, but to alert the Chaplain.

GILBERT

As to what?

HELEN

Why of our marriage, which, you know, must
take place today, Gilbert.

GILBERT

Your marriage? You an angel–you would marry
this accursed! Never! Never!

HELEN

Oh, Gilbert, my beloved, Gilbert, What are you
saying and of whom are you speaking?

GILBERT

I speak of Marsden, I speak of your fiancé. I tell you I must see him instantly without delay.

Ruthven returns.

RUTHVEN

What do you want with him, Count? Here he is!

GILBERT

Ah, it's him finally. Leave us, sister.

HELEN

Gilbert! George!

RUTHVEN

Stay, Miss!

GILBERT

Oh! You want–before her?

RUTHVEN

I have nothing to hide, my dear Gilbert, from the one who today shall be my wife.

GILBERT

Your wife? Oh! I really hope my sister's hand will never join with yours.

RUTHVEN

Moderate yourself, Count!

HELEN

Calm down a little, brother.

GILBERT

Be calm, be moderate–so be it, but let him
instantly get out of here never to reappear.

HELEN

My God!

RUTHVEN

Gilbert, my friend!

GILBERT

Oh, thank Heaven, I am not your friend. Thanks
to Heaven I don't know you, sir.

HELEN

But why do you want the Count to go away,
brother?

GILBERT

He doesn't ask me why–Go!

RUTHVEN

On the contrary, I was going to put that question,
Gilbert.

GILBERT

You are right, for it's necessary for my sister to
know the man to whom she's become so
imprudently engaged.

RUTHVEN

Oh! Oh!

HELEN

My God–what's going to happen?

GILBERT

Assassin of Juana, who do you want to kill here?

RUTHVEN

Assassin? Me? You know, Count, someone else
deserves that name more than I.

HELEN

Brother!

RUTHVEN

Which of us fell expiring at the foot of the
other? Speak, Count! Oh, you know I am not
angry with you about it. You know I've
pardoned you for it.

GILBERT

Yes, yes, I know that, but what I don't know, or
rather what I don't understand, is how you can
be living after my sword pierced your heart–how
you can be walking about when I myself lay you
on the ground, motionless, ice cold, dead!

HELEN

Oh!

RUTHVEN

It seems to me you had your explanation for that
yesterday.

GILBERT

Did you also explain why a man was waiting for
me in the thickets of Clisson and fired two
musket shots at me without hitting me? Did you
say who that man was?

RUTHVEN

Count, that resembles an accusation.

GILBERT

It is one. That man was you.

RUTHVEN

Me?

GILBERT

Assassin of Juana, why didn't you become the
assassin of Gilbert?

RUTHVEN

Me? And what interest would I have in killing
you, dear Gilbert–speak!

HELEN

Really, brother–

GILBERT

What interest? That of separating brother from
sister, when this brother arrived to defend his
sister, when this brother was going to tear his
sister from your hands. Don't you need two
virgins every year for your baneful life and your
bloody amours?

RUTHVEN

(aside)

He knows everything.

GILBERT

You don't reply, Milord.

RUTHVEN

What do you want me to say? You see him, dear
Helen. Well–what did I tell you?

HELEN

Alas! Alas! Poor Gilbert!

GILBERT

What! Helen, you hesitate despite what I just
told you? You don't shun this man with horror?
Oh, take care–for rather than let you be his prey,
you see, even here, in front of you–I will kill
him with my own hands.

HELEN

Brother! Brother!

GILBERT

Defend yourself, wretch–defend yourself for
when all is said and done, I don't assassinate!
I am not a Lord Ruthven.

RUTHVEN

Count–people are coming–they are going to hear
you.

GILBERT

Oh–let them come! Let them come! What I want
is for everyone to know you–what I want is for
them to hear me–Hola–everybody–everybody!

HELEN

Yes, yes, come! Help! Help!

RUTHVEN
(aside)
Bad luck, bad luck.

Gilbert runs to Lazare, who returns, along with some
peasants and servants.

GILBERT

Ah, come here, you! Do you recognize this
man?

LAZARE

Why, yes, Count, very well, very well!

GILBERT

Who is he?

LAZARE

He's my honored master.

GILBERT

Yes, but I am asking you something else. I am
asking you if I didn't draw my sword against
him in the ruins of Tormenar–pierce him to the
heart. He died in my arms–the same person who

GILBERT (cont'd)
had just killed the young Spanish girl, who had
just killed Juana?

LAZARE
(looking at Ruthven)
Huh?

RUTHVEN
Listen carefully, Lazare, and reply to the Count.
He asks you if you saw me kill Juana. Did you
see me kill Juana?

LAZARE
Oh, as to that, Count, no. Señora Juana was
killed but I don't know by whom.

GILBERT
(to Ruthven)
Oh, I say that it was by you, assassin.

RUTHVEN
The Count says that it was by me. I say, it was
by some bandits, your opinion, Lazare?

LAZARE
My opinion's the same as yours, sir.

GILBERT
Yes, I know very well no one was there and
consequently no one, except me, can affirm it.
But what you saw, Lazare–was this man
wounded, bloody–dead in my arms?

LAZARE

Oh–as to that, the fact is that I saw Milord very
low, very low, very low.

RUTHVEN

Doubtless he saw me faint.

GILBERT

Oh dead–quite dead I tell you.

RUTHVEN

Take care what you say, Count, for if this man
had seen me dead in Tormenar–he wouldn't be
seeing me living at Tiffauges–at least now
unless I am a ghost. Touch me, my friends, and
you will see.

GILBERT

(to Lazare)

Look here, wretch! Didn't you tell me yourself
you had seen a man waiting for me hidden in the
thickets of Clisson?

LAZARE

Ah, that, yes, that's true. I saw him as I see you,
Count.

RUTHVEN

But was I this man, Lazare?

LAZARE

Damn, I don't know, he had a mask on his face.

GILBERT

Yes, a mask, it's true, for you were afraid
someone would recognize you. And see,
my friends, it was a good precaution.

RUTHVEN

Well, I say you were in such fear that you saw
neither man nor mask–I say you only thought
you saw it–that's my opinion–take care, Lazare–
for what you say in reply is very important.

LAZARE

Damn–after all–I could be mistaken. Perhaps I
made a mistake, perhaps I didn't see anyone.

GILBERT

Oh!

HELEN

George, George–excuse him.

RUTHVEN

You see.

GILBERT

What! You doubt what I say? Between the word
of this man and mine, you hesitate? My friends,
my friends, I affirm to you on my soul that what
I've told you is true–that all was revealed to me
last night. I tell you a thing unheard of,
incredible, terrible–it's that this man is a demon!
That this man is a vampire! That his love is
death.

ALL

Ah!

HELEN

But who told you that, brother? Who told you that?

GILBERT

Melusina, the fairy of the Tapestry.

HELEN

My God!

GILBERT

My ancestors who were talking with her.

HELEN

My God! My God! Have pity, my poor brother is mad.

GILBERT

Me, mad?

HELEN

Oh, a doctor, a doctor for my poor Gilbert!

RUTHVEN

(to spectators)

You hear him, you see him, my friends. This is what we were trying to hide from. This is what the Count is forcing us to reveal to you despite ourselves.

GILBERT

Me, crazy? They think I'm crazy. I will become
so perhaps. So be it! But first–!

He rushes towards Ruthven.

HELEN

Help me, my friends!

The peasants and servants run and seize Gilbert.

RUTHVEN

My friends, in my name, in the name of
Countess Helen, in the name at once of a brother
and sister, take care of your master. Take him
away and take care that he not attempt suicide.

GILBERT

Assassin! Assassin!

RUTHVEN

If his reason is lost, let's at least save his life.

GILBERT

Helen! Helen!

HELEN

Yes, yes, my brother–don't worry, I won't leave
you.

RUTHVEN

That's right, Countess–accompany him–don't
leave him. The care of a sister will do more for
him than that of the best doctor. Oh, Gilbert!

RUTHVEN (cont'd)
Gilbert! I pity you sincerely, and I forgive you.
(to Lazare, giving him a purse)
Here, for you.

LAZARE
Ah, say, sir, it seems to me that I've been of
your opinion three or four times and that in this
purse at least.

RUTHVEN
Go—we'll settle up later.

They all leave except Ruthven.

RUTHVEN
Oh—this time Helen is really mine—and nothing
will tear her from me—when even her brother has
not been able to succeed. And now you, infernal
spirit who denounced me to Gilbert, you who
I recognized despite your disguise and your
trick—in the name of the Master who commands
us here and who has given equality to us and
power over mankind—spirit, my rival, appear—
I order you, appear even if you are at the
extremities of the world—appear!

Ziska—the Ghoul—appears.

ZISKA
Here I am—what do you want of me?

RUTHVEN

We are forbidden to betray each other to humans
and you have betrayed me.

ZISKA

No.

RUTHVEN

You lie! Yesterday night, I saw you disguised as
a Breton woman speaking to Gilbert.

ZISKA

Well?

RUTHVEN

The morning on the route to Clisson, you
warned him and you warded off my shots.

ZISKA

And so? To ward off the shots you fired–that's
my right. To take the costume of an old woman
and say, "Sleep in the chamber of the Tapestry
instead of sleeping in your room"–that's my
right again.

RUTHVEN

And why did you tell him that?

ZISKA

Because I love him.

RUTHVEN

You love–you? Do such as we love?

ZISKA

I love him, I tell you.

RUTHVEN

And you think he'll respond to your love?

ZISKA

I hope so.

RUTHVEN

You know that he loves a young girl–you know
he loves Antonia.

ZISKA

Yes, I know that! And, when we get to that love,
we shall see–meanwhile, it's a question of yours,
it's a question of his sister that he loves so much
that her death will kill him. Now, do you
understand, vampire? I want Gilbert to live.

RUTHVEN

Take care, I will tell him who you are!

ZISKA

And you will die then–that's our punishment if
we denounce one of our order–to become
mortal again.

RUTHVEN

Listen–it's noon. You know that I have only a
dozen hours to live without–

ZISKA

Yes–without Helen's blood.

RUTHVEN

Well–I want Helen. She's necessary to me!

ZISKA

And I–Gilbert is necessary to me–think how to
keep him living for me. By killing Helen, you
compromise Gilbert's life–think of that. I am
watching over him! I am there!

RUTHVEN

So–you want war?

ZISKA

No–I want love.

RUTHVEN

One last time–do you leave Helen to me?

ZISKA

One last time–will you leave me Gilbert?

RUTHVEN

No. You shall learn what I can be when I hate.

ZISKA

Fine. You shall learn what I can be when I love!

RUTHVEN

Adieu, Ghoul!

ZISKA

Au revoir–Vampire!

Blackout.

Scene VII

An apartment lit up for a party. Doors on each side–in the rear a large window giving on an abyss.

VASSALS
Long live the Count! Long live the Countess!

HELEN
Thanks, my friends, thanks.

RUTHVEN
(distributing money to them)
Here my friends, here.

PEASANT
May all the blessings of Heaven accompany you.

Eleven o'clock strikes.

RUTHVEN
(aside)
Eleven o'clock! Not a minute to lose! Till midnight.
(aloud)
Dear Helen, have you noticed that we haven't been alone for an instant all day long?

HELEN
Alas, dear George, today has been full of so many different things.

RUTHVEN

You will allow me to give these brave people their dismissal, won't you?

HELEN

Do it.

RUTHVEN

My friends, the Countess cannot be more appreciative of your friendship–but she is tired and she needs rest after all the emotions of this day.

JARWICK

We will retire, Milord.

ALL

Long live the Count! Long live the Countess!

They leave.

RUTHVEN

Ah, dear Helen! Finally, here we are alone!

HELEN

(pulling away, softly)

My friend, my dear George, you see I've fulfilled all the promises made–all the obligations undertaken.

RUTHVEN

Oh! Yes–and you are looking at the most happy of men!

HELEN

Are you the most happy of men, George? Oh–
if that's so, so much the better.

RUTHVEN

What! You doubt it, Helen?

HELEN

No–you say so and I believe you, but so close to
this happy man, George, there is another who is
very wretched.

RUTHVEN

Ah!

HELEN

You know of whom I speak–of poor Gilbert that
is kept out of view–of poor Gilbert who is mad
and who, in his madness, believes I am in danger
of death.

RUTHVEN

Helen, do you still have some doubts of me?

HELEN

Oh– God protect me from them! If I doubted
you, George–would you be my husband? No–
but I owe my brother some consolation. Let me
go see him, let me tell him that I am your wife,
let me calm him by telling him I'm happy.

RUTHVEN

Do as you like, Helen–you know best–you are
mistress, queen–but–

HELEN

What?

RUTHVEN

Listen, I'd prefer to go to him myself, attempt
one last effort, to say if necessary to Gilbert that
I renounce you, that I'm going away, that I'm
leaving–thus giving him peace of mind and with
peace of mind, life. It's a weakness, Helen, after
what you have just done for me, I know how
much you love me–but I also know how much
you love your brother, and I fear that his words,
although imprinted with the mark of madness,
will prejudice me in your eyes. You say this is
from a weak man? No, it's from a man who
loves.

HELEN

But if you don't succeed, George?

RUTHVEN

Then you will go yourself, Helen.

HELEN

So be it! Go, George.

RUTHVEN

Do you love me?

HELEN

George–to whoever I give my hand, I have given
my heart.

RUTHVEN

Oh–dear Helen! Wait for me–wait for me!

Exit Ruthven.

HELEN

(alone)

Who is this old woman to whom I gave alms and
who, as she accepted my money, said very low,
"Separate yourself for a moment from Lord
Ruthven–there's a man who has a revelation to
make to you." My God, you are witness that
I don't doubt him–but in spite of me, my
brother's words trouble me. Oh! He saw her,
poor George, and that's why he wanted to go to
Gilbert himself. Oh! How happy are girls who
have a mother. If I still had a mother, I would go
to her, I would tell her my anxiety, my anguish,
and she would counsel me–a mother's heart is
never deceived. Why, is it not for me as if my
mother was alive? Am I really one of those
pious girls who believes the soul never dies with
the body? Oh! Mother, so many times in that
silence and solitude, I've spoken to you as if you
were there. Oh! Mother, if my pious veneration
has brought me each day to your tomb with
flowers–as if the tomb were only a bed and
death but sleep–mother, if as I do not doubt,
your spirit watches over your daughter. Mother,
ask God–God who can refuse nothing to you–to
you, a saintly woman–ask God for a miracle and
manifest yourself to me–if not by yourself–
perhaps it is impossible, perhaps the eternal,
immutable laws of nature prevent your visible

HELEN (cont'd)
return to this world–at least through a human
way. Mother, tell me what I ought to fear, what
I ought to hope–my God, Lazare! Lazare! Have
you forsaken me, mother?

Lazare stands at the door, making a sign for Helen to
snuff the candles.

HELEN
What–you want me to snuff the candles?

LAZARE
Yes.

HELEN
And why do you want me to put them out?

LAZARE
Damn! Because I much prefer not to be seen
here.

HELEN
Why did you come here then?

LAZARE
Ah, damn, Miss–because, you see, I have a
conscience.

HELEN
A conscience! A conscience that drives you to
tell me something, right?

LAZARE

Yes.

HELEN

To make a confession to me?

LAZARE

Yes.

HELEN

Come then.

LAZARE
(gesturing to snuff the candles)
Pfoo! Pfoo! Then.

HELEN

So be it.
(she blows out the candles)
Ah, my God–what am I going to learn?

LAZARE

Where are you, Miss?

HELEN

Here.

LAZARE

Ah! What I have to say to you, you see, must be
said very near and very low.

HELEN

Good God!

LAZARE

Listen–since the scene a little while ago–I can
no longer see.

HELEN

Speak! Speak! I am listening!

LAZARE

From that moment, I've been watching.

HELEN

What?

LAZARE

That moment you would be alone.

HELEN

Well?

LAZARE

Well–I saw Milord go down to your brother and
at the risk of whatever might happen, I came up.

HELEN

Why?

LAZARE

To tell you that your brother–ah, My God–

HELEN

My brother–get to the point!

LAZARE

To tell you that your brother is not mad!

HELEN

Gilbert is not mad?

LAZARE

No–listen! To say that it was Milord, my master, who killed poor Juana–I don't dare. I wouldn't dare!

HELEN

Great God!

LAZARE

But that he died, and that he survived, I don't know how–oh, that I will swear to.

HELEN

Died?

LAZARE

Yes, died, dead, I know it quite well. I, who saw him carried, cold, icy on the rocks where he told them to put him–for you see, what he said very low to Count Gilbert, I heard perfectly–he said to him, "Count, I belong to a sect that does not bury its dead."

HELEN

My God! My God!

LAZARE

"At the time, I have uttered my last sigh–expose me in the air on a rock to the rays of the Moon." And that is what we did, unfortunately, instead

LAZARE (cont'd)
of stuffing him in a ditch a hundred feet deep
and piling all the stones of Tormenar on him.

HELEN
Then you believe, like Gilbert?

LAZARE
Yes.

HELEN
That he was dead?

LAZARE
Yes.

HELEN
And by some hellish miracle–?

HELEN
Yes.

HELEN
And that man yesterday–?

LAZARE
Yes.

HELEN
–Who wanted to kill my brother–?

LAZARE
Yes.

HELEN

You think also it was him?

LAZARE

Yes! Yes! Yes!

HELEN

But you told me the contrary before?

LAZARE

He had promised to make my fortune.

HELEN

Wretch!

LAZARE

He had given me this purse.

HELEN

Oh–for money–

LAZARE

I no longer want it, his money! I throw it away, I
renounce it. Oh, on my faith, I love my body,
but I have still greater care for my soul.

HELEN

Why then, Gilbert spoke the truth. I am lost–
I must flee–Ah! Silence!

LAZARE

It's him coming back!

HELEN

Help me, my God!

LAZARE

The door, the door!

He cannot find the door and hides in the window.

LAZARE

Five hundred feet! Oof!

Ruthven enters, carrying a candle.

RUTHVEN

Here I am, dear Helen! Your brother is more
peaceful–he's sleeping. I didn't wish to
reawaken him.
(looking at her)
How pale you are!

HELEN

Less than you, Milord!

RUTHVEN

Less than me? You know, Helen, that this pallor
is habitual with me–and it's quite simple–I lost
so much blood the day your brother almost
killed me.

HELEN

This pallor, excuse me, George, but it's the
pallor of a corpse and not of a living person.

RUTHVEN
What do you mean, Helen?

HELEN
I mean, Milord, that I come from valiant stock,
I mean that I've never been afraid–I mean that
you terrify me.

RUTHVEN
You too, Helen? Ah! This is what comes of
leaving you alone–solitude, silence, shadows–
have agitated your imagination. The shadows–
Why?–I left lights in this room before?

HELEN
In your absence, they were extinguished.

RUTHVEN
Oh–this is strange! All alone?

HELEN
All alone!

RUTHVEN
You are trembling, Helen.

HELEN
I told you–I'm afraid, I'm afraid.

He takes her hand.

HELEN
Cold like that of a cadaver.

RUTHVEN

Yes, cold, Helen, for your suspicion freezes me–
oh, come, come, my fiancée, my wife–come
against my breast–come against my heart!

HELEN

Oh–let me alone! It seems to me your breast is
not living–it seems to me your heart does not
beat!

RUTHVEN

Helen, Helen, someone has been here in my
absence–speak–tell me who has been here?

HELEN

No one! No one!

RUTHVEN
(looking around him)
Oh! Oh!
(stepping on Lazare's purse)
The purse I gave Lazare–the wretch has told all?
Treason! Treason!

HELEN

What do you say?

Ruthven goes to the doors and closes them.

RUTHVEN

Nothing! Nothing!

HELEN

Why are you closing that door?

RUTHVEN
Helen–aren't you my wife? Am I not your
husband?

HELEN
Milord! Milord!

Ruthven takes her in his arms.

HELEN
My brother! Gilbert!

LAZARE
(on the balcony)
Help! Help!

RUTHVEN
Ah! We are not alone here, it appears?

HELEN
Help! Help!

RUTHVEN
Oh! Call, call–fiancée of Ruthven, but when
they arrive–

HELEN
Help me!

RUTHVEN
Bad luck to you! Bad luck to your brother!

He drags her into the room on the side.

LAZARE

Help! Help!

GILBERT
(on the stairs)
Here I am! Here I am!
(he tries the door)
Oh, the door! The door!

LAZARE

Wait, wait, Count.

Lazare opens the door. Gilbert enters in the wildest disorder.

GILBERT

He had me chained, the wretch. I broke my
chains–he had me guarded by four men–I got
away from them and here I am! Where is my
sister–where is she?

LAZARE

There, sir, there!

Midnight begins to strike.

HELEN
(in the room)
Help me, Gilbert! I am dying–

GILBERT
(with a terrible yell)
Ah!

He rushes towards the door which opens. Ruthven appears. The two men, perceiving each other, utter a double shout. They hurl themselves at each other in a terrible embrace. Neither is armed. They try to choke each other. Gilbert drags Ruthven to the window.

RUTHVEN
Together then.

GILBERT
Yes, together, since I can annihilate you with me.

A struggle follows, in which Gilbert lifts Ruthven up; the two are about to fall over the balcony, when Lazare seizes a mace and strikes Ruthven.

Gilbert hurls him through the window–a great shout can be heard echoing through the depths of the chasm.

RUTHVEN
Ah!

After a moment's hesitation, Gilbert returns.

GILBERT
Sister, my sister!

He rushes to the side room–a scream can be heard.

GILBERT
Ah!

Blackout.

Scene VIII

The precipice. Ruthven's body is at the back of the chasm–broken by the fall. Gilbert is coming down the rocks, a torch in his hands.

He reaches Ruthven and examines the body with the aid of a torch.

GILBERT
Ah, this time the monster is indeed dead.

He goes back up several steps, then returns.

GILBERT
No matter.

He pushes a large rock and rolls it on top of Ruthven.

GILBERT
Ah, my sister, my sister. Have I really been able to avenge you?

CURTAIN.

Act V

Scene IX

The great hall in a palace in Circassia. In the rear, a terrace giving on immense gulf and on mountains. The stage is almost cut in half by tapestries which are closed.

At Rise, Lazare is standing behind Antonia; she is lying on a divan and fanned by slaves. They dance before her performing a Circassian dance to the sound of tambourines and guzlas.

After the dance, Lazare, Antonia and Ziska remain alone.

LAZARE
Well, Sultana Antonia, what do you say of the castle, the country and the people who inhabit it?

ANTONIA
I say, my dear Lazare, that, thanks to your efforts, I have been received here like a queen.

LAZARE
Say—thanks to the efforts of Ziska.

ANTONIA
(smiling at Ziska)
Is it then you I must thank, my beautiful Circassian?

Ziska makes a slight movement with her head.

LAZARE

Well, I hope that you no longer regret your villa at Spalatro, your mountains of Circassia and your Adriatic Sea? We have all this here–and on a grand scale–a Circassian palace–the Caucasus mountains–and the Black Sea.

ANTONIA

Lazare, I regret nothing if Gilbert arrives today as you promised me.

LAZARE

Listen, Sultana, he will be late a day or two, you mustn't be angry with him–it's a long way from the Chateau of Tiffauges to the fortress of Anabela and one cannot go from Brittany to Circassia like from Nantes to Clisson.

ANTONIA

Then he knows the country, my beloved Gilbert?

LAZARE

It appears he was here in his last voyage for he gave me exact information.

ANTONIA

And you are sure, Ziska, that this castle is indeed the one designated by Gilbert?

Ziska nods affirmatively.

ANTONIA

Fine–leave us.

Ziska leaves.

LAZARE

Huh! How erect these Circassians are!

ANTONIA

Never mind, Lazare. I find something strange
about this slave.

LAZARE

The eyes, right? Like me–it seems to me I've
already seen those eyes somewhere, but where,
I don't know at all.

ANTONIA

Lazare.

LAZARE

Signora?

ANTONIA

Do you know why Gilbert has demanded that
I leave Europe? Do you know why he begged
me to come here?

LAZARE

No–I know nothing about it.

ANTONIA

I understand that, after the death of his sister,
Brittany became odious to him, but still Europe

ANTONIA (cont'd)

is large and if he didn't wish to locate near me in
Italy, why not choose Spain?

LAZARE

Ah, well, yes, Spain! That's where we met.

ANTONIA

Or England?

LAZARE

England! Even less! That's where *he* came from.

ANTONIA

Eh? Why, of whom are you speaking, Lazare?

LAZARE

Of *him*, of course?

ANTONIA

Who is *he*?

LAZARE

Why, the enemy of the master.

ANTONIA

Gilbert has an enemy?

LAZARE

I think so, indeed! And who will be mine, too, if
he returns a second time.

ANTONIA

What do you mean, if he returns a second time?

LAZARE

The Count thinks he did a good job killing him this time–but yes, take care!

ANTONIA

Killed him? Gilbert killed a man? For goodness sake, what kind of story are you telling me, Lazare?

LAZARE

I know I really should not have spoken to you about this. Say, Signora, if my master never spoke to you of Lord Ruthven, don't speak of him, I beg you.

ANTONIA

Of Lord Ruthven?

LAZARE

Yes–it was the name of a person–oh–as to the rest, he was the last of his family, and he died intestate quite naturally. I found myself his heir– I've already seen about a quarter of a league from here, a charming house which I incessantly count on owning and, my word, if Ziska likes it, and you have nothing against this union–

ANTONIA

Me? My dear Lazare, on the contrary.

LAZARE

Well, then–it shall be done–meanwhile, if the Sultana has no need of me–?

ANTONIA

You will reclaim your liberty a bit, my dear
Lazare?

LAZARE

Oh! My God! Yes–a little visit to some brave
fishermen whose acquaintance I made three
months ago who have promised to find me a
very brave servant–you see, I wouldn't be sorry
to have a very brave servant to replace
Mr. Gilbert, who was a very brave master. I love
to have someone very brave around me. That
makes me even more brave. Anyway, that's it.
Should you have need of me, you can ask for me
by the seashore.

ANTONIA

Yes, go, my dear Lazare, go!

Exit Lazare.

ANTONIA

(alone)
Poor Lazare! I really think fear has slightly
turned his head. Happily, he brought a very
positive letter from Gilbert–

She pulls a letter from her breast which she reads.

ANTONIA (cont'd)

"Dear Antonia, if you love me, leave Spalatro,
leave Dalmatia, leave Europe, follow the honest
lad I send you. Stop where he stops and wait for
me–Perhaps you will risk your life and mine in

ANTONIA (cont'd)

not fulfilling to the letter the prayer I place very
humbly at your cherished feet–All that can be
told of our misfortunes, Lazare will tell you.
I will be with you on the 15th of March." Today
is the 15th of March–unless there's an accident
or ill luck, I will see him again today. Only
where will he come from? Two roads are open
to him–sea and mountain. If he's coming by sea,
I already would have noticed on the blue horizon
the sail of his ship. Oh, I much prefer that my
Gilbert not come by sea–these coasts are filled
with so many reefs. And then, these are the
waves which seem to predict a storm–happily
the horizon is empty. Nothing but the white
spot–the wing of a sea bird, no doubt, or at most,
the sail of a fisherman fleeing the storm. Oh–
hasten to return poor bark lost in space, for now
the sea is beginning to undulate under the breath
of the wind. Oh! My beloved Gilbert, come by
way of the mountain, I beg you! Use intrepid
mules and spirited horses, but don't use the
waves–the calmest waves cover an abyss. Oh!
That little white spot is getting larger on the
horizon. I was mistaken. It's not a sea bird–I was
mistaken, it's not a sail of a fishing boat–it's a
bold ship coming from Europe. How large it's
getting–how it comes on! It seems to go faster
than the copper-colored wave which pursues it
in the heaven. Oh! The storm will reach it, poor
boat, before it gets to port. My Lord God, let
Gilbert not be one of the passengers! Gilbert, my
dear soul! Gilbert! My Gilbert!

Suddenly, the tapestry rises and Gilbert appears.

> GILBERT
> You are calling for me, Antonia?

> ANTONIA
> (turning)

Ah!

She runs to throw herself in his arms.

> GILBERT
> You! You! Finally, dear love! You, the only happiness in my life.

> ANTONIA

Gilbert.

> GILBERT
> You've come then?

> ANTONIA
> You commanded and your creature obeyed.

> GILBERT
> Without resistance, without regrets?

> ANTONIA
> Oh—with a thread from the Virgin, your love will lead me to the end of the world.

> GILBERT
> Then you are ready?

ANTONIA

Didn't I say I was waiting for you?

GILBERT

Right, right–today even, you will be mine. This
very night–you will have made me forget my
shame–you will have bound up my wounds.

ANTONIA

Gilbert, they say that wounds of the heart must
not heal too quickly, for if they do, they leave
nasty scars–the blood must be stopped but must
be cooled with tears. Weep, Gilbert, weep–or
rather let us weep–our sister, Helen, is dead.

GILBERT

Oh, no, no, on the contrary, Antonia, let's speak
no more of Helen–make me forget the six
months of my life that have just elapsed. Since
we last met, Helen has gone to Heaven to rejoin
Juana–and I have up there two angels to pray for
me, Antonia. There are some souls whose heart
is the only true home.

ANTONIA

Gilbert, God who gives us love, makes a Heaven
for us on Earth where he sends me to tell you–
Helen and Juana are happy–be happy.

GILBERT

Ah! If you could read in my heart, Antonia, you
would see only love and joy. I'm an ingrate, an
egoist, I forget the dead. I disdain the living.
Antonia, I have only one thought: You. Only

GILBERT (cont'd)

one hope: You. Only one desire: You. I efface
all the somber pages of my past life. I am born
again today, Antonia. Today is my first Sun, my
first smile, my first love.

ANTONIA

Oh, Gilbert, I am ravished to hear you talk this
way. How content I am to have to obey you–
How proud I am to run where you will call me–
your desire, your approval! So, the worry whose
cause you haven't told has dissipated–right? So
you no longer dread anything? Our flight to
these mountains frees us from the unknown
danger which threatens your life and mine and
you have discovered this corner of the world
where we can live unknown and happy?

GILBERT

Oh, yes, happy! Happy! Especially if we are
ignored.

ANTONIA

Happy! Happy! I intend to lull with that word
stamped with the language of angels. Antonia
happy because of Gilbert–Gilbert happy because
of Antonia.

GILBERT

Look at the heavens, look at this little blue
corner where it can still be found and which
reflects itself in my eyes and my heart. Well, it
is the image of felicity which has been granted
me. No, Antonia never has more pure joy been

GILBERT (cont'd)

given to a man than that which God grants me in
this moment. But this joy is lacking only one
thing–it's that instead of calling you my fiancée,
I may call you my wife. Take care, Antonia! The
time we are losing in desiring happiness, God
himself in all his power cannot return to us.
I come after six months, Antonia, and I ask why
you are not yet my wife.

ANTONIA

Gilbert, give your fiancée a quarter of an hour to
change from her mourning. Do you want me to
go to the altar to thank God in the lugubrious
apparel of an orphan or widow? Oh, no, no,
Gilbert, these veils will bring us bad luck–and
yet, if you demand it, I will obey–believe me, at
the moment I say yes, I'll have enough joy in my
heart that my black robe will shine like a feast
dress. But it's a holy custom of my country that
the bride resemble the Madonna–and if you
really want it, Gilbert–

GILBERT

Go warn the Priest.

ANTONIA

Yes. I will run there!

GILBERT

Make yourself beautiful and since we are happy,
there's to be no more mourning; neither in our
clothes or in our hearts or in Heaven.

There is a roll of thunder.

> ANTONIA
>
> Listen! Listen the storm! Oh! You did well to come by the mountains. God be blessed who raises the sea, but only when I hold you safely in my arms.

> GILBERT
>
> Ah, yes, a storm, it's true.

> ANTONIA
>
> Gilbert, see the ship which is trying to reach port?

> GILBERT
>
> Are there still wretches who suffer and who tremble? I'd forgotten!

> ANTONIA
>
> Oh, let's think only of ourselves, Gilbert.

She claps her hands.

> GILBERT
>
> What are you doing?

> ANTONIA
>
> I'm calling my women. I don't want to leave you.

The slaves–including Ziska–enter silently.

GILBERT

Oh! You won't leave me anymore, be easy.
            (recognizing Ziska)
Ah!

ANTONIA

What is it?

GILBERT

Who is this woman?

ANTONIA

This is Ziska, the Circassian. She guided Lazare
in his investigations and prepared everything
here for my arrival.

GILBERT

It's strange—it seems to me I've already seen
her—that I already know her.

ANTONIA

This is not the first time you've been here so it
could be you've seen her.

GILBERT

Yes, yes, you're right—go and return as quickly
as possible.

ANTONIA

Oh—a white dress and some roses. I will be
beautiful and you will love me Gilbert for my
principal beauty will be my love—for my richest
dress will be my happiness. Au revoir, my love!

She leaves.

GILBERT
(marching straight to Ziska)
You are shaking, you went pale–you are
trembling?

ZISKA
Yes.

GILBERT
Your eye threatened Antonia?

ZISKA
Yes.

GILBERT
You hate her?

ZISKA
Yes.

GILBERT
Look, I confess that I know you–I confess that
I've seen you–but where or when, my God?

ZISKA
Ingrate.

GILBERT
Ah, you are the Breton woman from the thickets
of Clisson, right? The one who saved my life–
the one who forewarned me of the danger my
poor sister ran.

ZISKA

It's nice you remembered.

GILBERT

What kind of creature are you to be able to so
change your costume, your abode and your
very appearance?

ZISKA

Alas, but I cannot change my heart!

GILBERT

Why are you everywhere I am?

ZISKA

You don't divine, Gilbert?

GILBERT

No.

ZISKA

I love you!

GILBERT

You love me! You!

ZISKA

Yes. Well, have you nothing to say to me in
return, Gilbert?

GILBERT

Nothing except that you frighten me.

ZISKA

Is that your only response?

GILBERT

And what other response could you expect from
me?

ZISKA

Take care, Gilbert! I've crossed mountains,
rivers, kingdoms to follow you–I have watched
over each of your steps. I've done everything for
you that a lover can do.

GILBERT

You didn't save my sister.

ZISKA

Oh–I would have saved her, if it had been
permitted to me. Look–look at me, Gilbert? Do
you think you cannot love me?

GILBERT

How can you ask me that, since you know my
love for Antonia?

ZISKA

Gilbert, I am immortal and I don't understand
loves that pass.

GILBERT

Then keep your love for a god and don't come
offer it to a man.

ZISKA

Why not, if I can make that man a god? Why, if with a ray of my immortality, I can make that man the king of the world and terrestrial creatures.

GILBERT

I love Antonia.

ZISKA

Reflect! You are both young–I know it, you are both good-looking, I know that, too. But what does youth or beauty count compared to eternity? Two flowers will last a springtime; two roses that fade in winter shed their leaves with age. Devouring years pass like a breeze over your head and you will find yourselves, old wrinkled, staggering, hardly strong enough to support the memory of your beautiful years. Look, Gilbert, aren't you ambitious? Speak–do you refuse eternal youth, eternal power, eternal love? Oh, we love well too, we, supernatural creatures, and all your life of mortal happiness with Antonia will last no longer than a kiss in our immortal delirium.

GILBERT

Oh, woman, you attack me exactly where I am invulnerable. You forget that I've seen all those that I loved die–my father, my mother, my sister–I don't wish to see Antonia die–I want to walk with her, by equal steps, to the tomb. Love to me is sweeter with a mortal because it will last a very short time. Yes, I know our love, to

GILBERT (cont'd)

other men, resembles those flowers which turn
to fruits which once ripe, fall into dust, but what
do you expect! The flower enchants me,
especially because its stem is bowing, because
its perfume wends away, because its luster
fades. I am accustomed to pity and to love; to
esteem, the joy in proportion to the pain–love
then, someone other than me, woman, you can
see clearly I cannot love you.

ZISKA

So you mortals call being happy, not suffering
completely.

GILBERT

Listen–I don't know what I call happy–I know I
am happy–that's all.

ZISKA

Oh–because you take a chimera for happiness?

GILBERT

If I see her that way and if she suffices for my
soul–leave her to me, Ziska!

ZISKA

No–for your chimera makes me pity–poor fool
that you are.

GILBERT

My heart is screaming in joy and you want to
make me believe I am wretched? Fool, it's you!

ZISKA

Gilbert, you have the shadow–I offer you the
reality.

GILBERT

What do you want me to say to you? I love
Antonia–if you are as powerful as you say, make
me love you.

ZISKA

Oh! Wretch, be kind to me!

GILBERT

Don't poison my happiness and I will be kind to
you.

ZISKA

Your happiness.

GILBERT

Yes.

ZISKA

Alas!

GILBERT

You pity me?

ZISKA

Alas!

GILBERT

What do you mean to say?

ZISKA

I mean to tell you that, an hour ago, the sky was
pure. See the sky, Gilbert.

GILBERT

My God, let that attempt shatter the Heavens–
the growling of thunder cannot choke the joyous
voice of love which surges in my heart.
Goodbye! I am going to the chapel.

He rushes outside. Ziska sits down. The storm breaks out
with fury.

Lazare enters, accompanied by some fishermen.

LAZARE

The ship is wrecked–the wretches are going to
perish–go my friends, go! Try to save some of
them. Run the risk, my friends, run the risk!

The fishermen leave.

LAZARE

Me, I cannot. My responsibilities attach me to
the shore. Ah, my God, there's yet one sloop
that founders. The last hope of these poor folk.
Yes, swim–it's as if you couldn't swim! Ah–so!
But, Lazare, it's you who are a rogue, you are
a coward! What! You will let these unfortunates
perish without trying to save even one at least?
And if your master, your unfortunate master,
were among the shipwrecked? Ah! There's

223

LAZARE (cont'd)
another one disappearing. Brr! Good. There's
another one swimming this way. Wait, wait, I'm
going to do something good. I'm going to
redeem some sins...

He pulls down a cord.

LAZARE
Let's see!

He throws it over the parapet of the terrace.

LAZARE
Fine–that works–that holds well.
(pulling)
Huh? Huh? Poor man, go! All men are brothers.
Eh?
(pulls)
Come, my brother, come, my fellow creature,
come.

Suddenly, he notices the head of Ruthven, which appears
facing him.

LAZARE
Ha!

The vampire clings to the terrace. Lazare rushes at him
and throws him into the sea. Then, trembling, he stag-
gers and babbles.

LAZARE
Help! Help!

Gilbert returns.

GILBERT

What's the matter?

LAZARE

Ah! Sir! Sir!

GILBERT

What?

ZISKA

We are lost.

GILBERT

Lost?

LAZARE

I saw him.

GILBERT

Who?

LAZARE

Milord! Him! Him! The vampire!

GILBERT

Ah!

LAZARE

Let's escape, Milord. Let's escape! Pardon me,
I am mistaken. I just called you Milord, but I'm
out of my head–

GILBERT

You saw this man again?

LAZARE

There–like I see you. I threw him back in the water–you understand clearly that I pushed him–he fell back in the sea–but that accomplishes nothing, you know him–the bastard. Oh, sir, let's escape! In the name of Heaven–let's escape!

GILBERT

Oh, my God! My God! My God!

LAZARE

Sir! Sir!

GILBERT

Go!

LAZARE

I have so much fear that I dare not escape without you. Oh, my teeth are chattering. Ta, ta, ta–

GILBERT

That's fine–go away–I'll stay.

LAZARE

Oh, sir, yes, stay–stop him if you can–retain him if you can–that will let us gain a little time, sir. I'm escaping.

He runs off.

ZISKA

Well, Gilbert, where is your happiness? Where
is this beautiful fruit flower which must ripen?

GILBERT

Oh, you are immortal, you said so, and as for
some time I've seen things so incredible, so
strange that I don't doubt it–Ziska, you are
everything and I am nothing. Ziska, I fall at your
knees–you see, you must pardon this weak mind.
This laughable weakness, this wretch, this atom,
this grain of dust that in its pride, believed
himself a mountain. Pardon, Ziska–I am
humbling myself–oh, spare me–help me!

ZISKA

Willingly.

GILBERT

You offered me your life?

ZISKA

Yes.

GILBERT

You've asked me to renounce Antonia?

ZISKA

Yes.

GILBERT

I consent to everything. Take me, I belong to
you. But you understand that I must not see a

GILBERT (cont'd)
third victim dying in my arms–that I cannot bear
the death rattle of a third in agony–that this
creature, so much loved, that this virgin, pure,
not leave me alone, desolated, overwhelmed on
the Earth. Ziska, save Antonia–save my fiancée.
Defend her against the vampire. Let her live,
and as for me, you shall take me and I will bless
you for having taken me from Antonia. But let
her live. Let her live!

ZISKA
Impossible, Gilbert.

GILBERT
Impossible? Why, you lied then. You cannot
save this young girl–you cannot tear her from
her hideous enemy, for it's she–it's she he's
come looking for–you cannot make her live–and
you came to me to speak of your power–of your
immortality. The only gift I ask of you, you
refuse–and you come to me to speak of your
love! Look, think carefully, reflect well–before
answering me.

ZISKA
Impossible.

GILBERT
Fine! Another thing!

ZISKA
What?

GILBERT

Oh, something that will be in your power, this
time, I hope–Ziska, I ask you for death for her
and me.

ZISKA

So, you love her to the point of dying with her?

GILBERT

Yes, I had consented to live without her–if she
was living–if she dies, I want to die.

ZISKA

So be it! What type of death do you choose?

GILBERT

Give us a poison that strikes like lightning in a
kiss.

ZISKA

Oh!

GILBERT

You hesitate?

ZISKA
(giving him a small bottle)
No, here.

GILBERT

Be blessed.

ZISKA

How happy he is! How happy she is!

She notices Gilbert's sword dropped on an armchair–she seizes it and leaves rapidly.

GILBERT
(alone)
Oh, yes, yes, death, repose–after fatigue, after sadness, after the catastrophe of my cursed destiny. Really, what's there to do and what's the use of struggling? What's the good of shutting him back in a tomb that always reopens? Oh, no, no–I don't want to see him again–I wish to forestall his presence. And she who knows nothing, who doubts nothing, she who, all this time–Antonia, Antonia, my love.

Antonia enters dressed in white, completely happy.

ANTONIA
Have I been long, and am I really beautiful?

GILBERT
Oh–misfortune!

ANTONIA
My God! How pale you are!

GILBERT
Yes, I am pale, for I am a wretch. Just now I promised you love, happiness, a future. I lied. None of all that is for us. I come, I bring you death. I wanted to involve you in my destiny; now, you are cursed as I am cursed. No more

GILBERT (cont'd)

flowers, no more fancy dress, no more joy, no more anything. Yes, I am pale, Antonia, I am like one is when one is going to die.

ANTONIA

To die? You are going to die, my Gilbert?

GILBERT

Yes, a terrible fate has beaten me. All those I love fall victim to a monster who pursues me. It's a horrible secret–but you must know it.

ANTONIA

My God! What was Lazare saying of this man, this Englishman, this Ruthven?

GILBERT

Antonia, in Spain, I acted as a protector of a young girl named Juana. Juana died in front of my eyes–butchered. In Brittany where, you know, I was recalled by my sister, I saw her die in the same way. I come here, I hold you in my arms, I love you–to the end of the world, the monster follows me–he's here. He's going to come. He's coming.

ANTONIA

Why this man–he's–

GILBERT

He's a vampire.

ANTONIA

Ah–but you won't leave me, you will defend
me–you will kill him?

GILBERT

Antonia, this hand has laid him in the tomb
twice.

ANTONIA

Let us flee! Flee!

GILBERT

Wherever we shall go–he will follow us.

ANTONIA

Hide me in some unknown retreat, in some
unknown subterranean place–so long as I see
you, so long as you are near me, I will be happy
anywhere, anywhere!

GILBERT

Useless! His eye will discover you in the most
profound abyss of this Earth. Antonia! Antonia!
Do you love me?

ANTONIA

Oh!

GILBERT

Could you live without me?

ANTONIA

Not an hour! Not a minute!

GILBERT

Well, a refuge remains to us: death.

ANTONIA

With you? With you?

GILBERT

Yes.

ANTONIA

Ah, you've often said to me, "Antonia give me
proof that you love me." Gilbert my beloved,
you are going to have this proof. I am ready!
Are you ready?

GILBERT

My love, my unique treasure, my only soul–
you've often asked me if your love was joy–
well, judge what your love is to me–swear this
death is still the supreme happiness.

Antonia tries to take the poison.

GILBERT

Oh–relax–I won't make you wait. Your hand in
mine, Antonia–my look plunging into your
heart, your lips on my lips so that I can breath
your last breath while giving you my last sigh–
come, Antonia, come!

He takes her in his arms. Ziska reappears and tears the
bottle from his hands.

ZISKA

Stop!

ANTONIA

Ziska!

GILBERT

Behind me, demon–since you cannot make us
live, let us at least die!

ZISKA

Oh–don't rush to suspect and curse, Gilbert.

ANTONIA

What's she saying?

ZISKA

Young girl, I must speak to your fiancé.

ANTONIA

To Gilbert?

ZISKA

Yes.

ANTONIA

Well, speak.

ZISKA

I have to speak to him alone.

ANTONIA

Oh! Gilbert, I won't leave you.

ZISKA
Gilbert–order her to leave us together.

ANTONIA
Gilbert, I am afraid.

GILBERT
And if he, meanwhile–

ZISKA
He can do nothing to her until midnight–until
midnight I will answer for everything.

GILBERT
Oh–by what oath can you assure me?

ZISKA
By my love, Gilbert. I swear to you here until
midnight, no harm will come to Antonia.

GILBERT
Antonia, leave us.

ANTONIA
Gilbert, it's you who wish it?

ZISKA
Go, little girl, and don't come back until you are
called.

GILBERT
Obey, my Antonia.

ANTONIA

Gilbert.

GILBERT

Go, dear love, go. What have we to fear? Are we
not sure of dying together?

Antonia leaves.

GILBERT (cont'd)

Well, we are alone–speak–I am listening.

ZISKA

She consented to die? With you?

GILBERT

Is she worthy of my love, Ziska?

ZISKA

I don't find the sacrifice very great, Gilbert.

GILBERT

Why's that?

ZISKA

To die in your arms, to die on your heart hearing
you murmur, "I love you." Oh, no–why haven't
you asked such a little thing of me, Gilbert? Oh,
I would die in your arms with delight.

GILBERT

Why do you speak of dying since you are
immortal?

ZISKA

Yes–that's true–anyway, this is not what I have
to tell you.

GILBERT

What thing have you to tell me? Hurry up then.

ZISKA

Well, Gilbert, being unable to die with you–I
don't wish you to die.

GILBERT

But Antonia! Antonia!

ZISKA

Antonia–Antonia won't die either.

GILBERT

What are you saying?

ZISKA

There's a way to save her.

GILBERT

Oh–why didn't you say that when it was a
question of my sister?

ZISKA

Because I knew you would live, even if your
sister died–just as I know that if Antonia dies,
you will die.

GILBERT

Wait! Look–I don't quite understand.

ZISKA

I am saying that you are going to live, Gilbert,
and live happily.

GILBERT

With Antonia.

ZISKA

With Antonia.

GILBERT

Oh, no, no. I don't dare believe it, no, you said
before it's impossible.

ZISKA

If I save her, Gilbert, if I make you so happy, at
the expense of–

GILBERT

Of what? Speak.

ZISKA

No, of nothing. If I make you so happy–will you
always hate me?

GILBERT

Me, hate you? Oh, till my last day, till my last
hour, to my last sigh, I will bless you.

ZISKA

Gilbert! Gilbert! Never mind–even were you to
hate me–even were you to forget me–which
would be even worse, I will save you.

GILBERT
With her? With Antonia?

ZISKA
Yes, with her–with Antonia, but don't deprive
me of my strength by repeating that name too
often.

GILBERT
Well, look–what must be done?

ZISKA
Combat him and strike him.

GILBERT
Oh–I've already struck him down twice.

ZISKA
Yes, but with human arms.

GILBERT
But with what arms do you want me to hit him?

ZISKA
Ruthven is a demon–take the Lord with you–and
you will conquer Ruthven.

GILBERT
Explain!

ZISKA
Listen–you left your sword on that chair. I took
it and gave it to Lazare. A Priest was waiting to

ZISKA (cont'd)

marry you. Gilbert, get him to bless your sword.
Take this holy sword, Gilbert, and present the
point to Ruthven–before it, he will recoil–strike
him with this sword and the wound–be it as light
as that made by a needle on the finger of a
child–that wound will kill him.

GILBERT

Oh, thanks, thanks–but what's wrong with you,
Ziska? You are staggering.

ZISKA

You don't grasp it, Gilbert?

GILBERT

No.

ZISKA

You don't grasp that, as you have refused my
immortality, I am giving you my death?

GILBERT

Your death?

ZISKA

You don't understand that we are linked by
terrible laws–you don't grasp that I cannot
betray him except at the expense of my own
immortality. I have betrayed him and I am
dying.

GILBERT

Ziska!

ZISKA

And I am dying alone–I am dying to make you
happy with my rival. Finally, you understand,
Gilbert–which of us loves the best–Antonia or I?

GILBERT

Oh! Ziska.

He takes her hand.

ZISKA

Thank you.
             (she kisses his hand)
And now, goodbye for this world, goodbye for
the other, goodbye for eternity.

She disappears in flames.

GILBERT
(with a terrible cry)

Ah!

Antonia returns and falls to her knees.

ANTONIA

Ah!

The horn sounds.

GILBERT

The first stroke of midnight. Not an instant to
lose–the sword! The sword!

He rushes out.

ANTONIA
(alone)
My God! What's happening? My legs fail me. It
seems as if an invisible enemy is approaching.

She looks to the side, towards the door.

ANTONIA
Ah!

Ruthven enters.

ANTONIA
Gilbert! Help me, Gilbert!

Enter Gilbert, sword in hand.

GILBERT
Come to me, Ruthven, come to me!

RUTHVEN
You again!

GILBERT
Yes, only this time I come in the name of the
Lord!

ANTONIA
(enveloping Gilbert in her arms)
Gilbert, my Gilbert.

GILBERT
Cursed creature! Do you renounce Satan?

RUTHVEN

No.

GILBERT

Demon, do you confess to God?

RUTHVEN

No.

GILBERT

One more time, answer!

RUTHVEN

No.

GILBERT

Well, you are going to die forever–forever
cursed and despairing.

RUTHVEN
(roaring)

Ah!

He recoils slowly before the sword as Gilbert advances.
Arriving near the wall, both go out through it.

Lazare appears and supports Antonia who is ready to
faint.

Blackout.

Scene X

A cemetery. Tombs, cypresses, sinister and fantastic background–snow on the ground–red Moon in the sky.

Enter Gilbert, backing Ruthven into an open tomb.

GILBERT
For the last time, worship God!

RUTHVEN
No.

GILBERT
Then despair and die!

He buries the sword in the vampire's heart.

Ruthven falls in the open ditch letting out a shout, the stone cover falls back of itself and shuts him in.

GILBERT
In the name of the Lord, Ruthven, I seal you in this tomb for eternity!

He traces a cross on the stone, which becomes luminous.

At that moment, the sky fills with angels. Helen and Juana detach themselves and come to find Ziska, who rises from the ground, hands extended to Heaven. Antonia appears and rushes into Gilbert's arms.

HELEN
Brother, be happy!

JUANA
(to Antonia)
Sister, be happy.

CURTAIN.

Entretien with a Vampire

by

Frank J. Morlock

"Alexander, I've come to die."

My father's words chilled me, as his giant frame stood in my doorway, but of course, I made him welcome.

His enormous body, seemingly indestructible was succumbing to a series of small strokes. The inevitable dissolution would take several months, and medicine could do nothing; the only thing was to make him as comfortable as possible.

We talked a lot: about his place in literature and the many books he had written. He finally reread *The Three Musketeers* that he had first written in 1845, and which had changed him from France's leading romantic playwright into a world famous novelist and a fabulously rich man.

"What did you think of it after rereading it?"

"I think it's pretty good."

There were many other topics of conversation, some quite painful involving our personal relationship. My father seemed perfectly lucid in every respect right up until his death. He sat in a chair and was able to watch the beach at Dieppe from my garden.

But there was one thing that made me question his sanity. He began to talk of vampires.

"Beware of vampires, *fils*."

"Of course, *père*."

"You think I'm mad or joking. I'm neither. Be especially on your guard against Lord Ruthven or whatever he's calling himself today He uses many aliases."

"Lord Ruthven–didn't you write a play about him?"

"Yes, and it cost me my fortune."

"I rather thought you went into bankruptcy because you were over-extended."

"That's what everyone thought. Poor old Dumas, he's a spendthrift; he cannot keep track of money and he went bust."

"Yes, we all thought that."

"That's what they wanted you to think. But the truth was that I was the victim of a sinister vampire plot to make it appear that way."

Now I knew my father was mad. I wanted to tell him to stop, to reason with him, but he halted my burgeoning protests with a gesture and went on.

"It's true that I had large debts *in toto*. But they were all small, and I could keep paying them off with royalties from a new book or a new play. I'd been doing it for years. In that case, what happened was that those accursed vampires went around buying them all up. Once they had enough, they demanded payment in concert, and of course, I couldn't pay them all and I had to flee to Brussels."

"Yes, but father who–why would vampires want to ruin you, the great Alexandre Dumas?"

"Because I tried to expose them."

"I don't understand."

"Vampires are everywhere, Alexandre! They feed on us and they have to live amongst us. It's the only way they can live. But the trick of the thing is to keep it quiet. If the public knew the extent of the infestation, they would demand that it be rooted out. So vampires try to 'live' as inconspicuously as possible."

"All this is—"

"Very strange, I agree. We're taught not to believe in vampires. Who do you suppose benefits from that? It's all part of the conspiracy. Once you realize that vampires are real, you look at the world differently. Things that seemed inexplicable or the result of mere chance become plain and simple—and connected. So watch out for Lord Ruthven or Sir Williams, as he calls himself, and his henchmen and friends, Rocambole and Baccarat."

"I never play Baccarat."

"Baccarat is a woman from the *demi-mondaine* as you so aptly coined the term."

"Ah, like my Camille."

"Yes, and now that you mention it, they killed her, too. Or more precisely made her one of them."

"What! Impossible!"

"I'll explain it all to you later. Right now, I feel very tired, and I need some sleep."

I was glad enough to terminate the conversation. I was certain my father had gone mad. We never spoke of Camille again and I had no desire to bring the subject up again. It brought me too much pain. I put it down to the ravings of a dying man, who was very dear to me despite all the difficulties we had had in our personal relationship over the years. My illegitimacy and his refusal to marry my mother was a recurring, indeed an endless irritant. Still we loved each other.

After the funeral, I went through his effects mechanically; and, carefully hidden, I found a meticulously wrapped manuscript. I thought it might have been a new novel he was working on as I unwrapped it. My shock was considerable when I read the title: *A True Account of My Struggle Against the Vampire Ruthven & Several of His Human Accomplices.*"

Opening it, I began to read the memoirs of my father.

'Vampires are real, Alexandre,' said Victor Hugo.
'Bah!'
'The battle between humans and vampires has been going on for centuries.'
'In a figurative sense, yes, Victor.'
'No. In a literal sense, Alexandre.'
'But...'
'And in this battle, the Priory of Sion has been in the vanguard.'
'Ah, yes, your famous Priory, Victor!'
'Scoffer.'
'No. I know the Priory exists. Charles Nodier, who was a dear friend of mine, was its head, and now you. I know all that. But after all, what is it? What has it done?'
'You know that, of necessity, my lips are sealed, Alexandre,' replied Hugo.
'And you are asking me to believe, Victor?'
'I insist that you believe!'
'In the Priory?'
'Yes!'
'In an ongoing battle with vampires?'
'Centuries long.'
'And who's winning?'
'So far–a stalemate. But the battle continues and the enemy is relentless, cunning and, in a sense, immortal.'
'How can you expect anyone to believe this?'
'I'm not asking anyone, Alexandre... I am asking

you, my friend and acolyte, and when I say on my word of honor–'

'Very well, Victor–I accept what you say–though my mind rebels.'

'Your mind must be engaged in the battle. I am calling on you, Alexandre Dumas, né *de la Paillery, to give battle like a good Christian knight against evil!'*

'Well, what precisely do you want me to do?'

'For a start. write a play about vampires. Let the world be aware!'

'I'm willing enough to do that. But it seems to me that Nodier already wrote a play 20 years ago.'

'True enough.'

'Based on Byron's story.'

'Polidori's actually...'

'In any case, why another play?'

'Nodier wrote one, it's true. But Nodier is not the dramatist you are, Alexandre. The public must never be allowed to forget that these creatures walk amongst us.'

There was a long pause.

Well, as to writing a play–willingly... Vampires, after all, might make a good subject for drama, all be it, of the sensational kind

'I agree. You shall have your play in a week.'

'You can write a play in a week?'

'Certainly. It rarely takes longer once I've got the idea in my head.'

'It takes me rather longer.'

'But you are a great poet, Victor.'

'And you?'

'I'm a vulgarizer.'

It took, in fact, a bit longer than I expected because other matters intervened, but I soon returned with the play to Victor's home, and after a very fine dinner, I read it to him.

'Well, what do you think?'

'Powerful.'

'Better than Nodier?'

'Much better–and I'm not disparaging Nodier's achievement, either. It's a great play.'

'Do you suggest any changes?'

'No–just get it before the public as soon as possible. These creatures are becoming very powerful. Soon it may be too late to expose them.'

'Well, I'll take it around to Harel. I think he'll be interested. There'll be no trouble in putting it on.'

'Don't be so sure...'

At this point, I stopped reading from my father's manuscript and reflected.

Victor Hugo, my father's friend and rival, and Charles Nodier, another old friend and mentor of my father? Battling vampires! It all seemed so absurd!

And yet, I did recall that Nodier was the head of some obscure society called The Priory of Sion indeed, and that Victor Hugo had succeeded him as the head of this shadowy organization. And then I remembered at various places in my father's works were scattered obscure references to a Priory of Sion... What did he know about this secret society? Was he a member? Was he trying to give information about it?

It was all very strange but I was looking at my father's work in an entirely new–and eerie–light.

I went back to the manuscript.

For a number of reasons that I didn't pay much attention to at the time, events kept putting off the staging of Le Vampire. *At first, Harel was interested, but then he suddenly changed his mind. Indeed, there was a pattern but I didn't recognize it. Finally, after the success of* Monte-Cristo, *I decided I was ready to stage* Le Vampire. *I let it be known I was looking for a theatre. Not long after that Joseph, my valet, announced:*

'Two gentlemen to see you, sir.'

'Their names?'

'They didn't give any.'

'Bill collectors?'

'I don't think so, sir, but I don't really like the looks of them.'

'Show them in.'

They were two tall men in black whose clothes seemed to fit them ill, like pallbearers.

'Monsieur Dumas?'

'Yes?'

'Forgive our intrusion but we understand that you've written a new play?'

'It's true.'

'About vampires?'

'Yes.'

'Lord Ruthven?'

'Yes.'

'And you intend to put it on?'

'Absolutely.'

'Where?'

'That's a good question. No producer seems interested.'

'You won't be able to put that play on in any theatre in Paris, or in France for that matter.'

'I take it you have something to do with it?'

'Yes.'

'Hum!'

'Monsieur Dumas, we realize you write for money

and that, with your expenses and lavish lifestyle, you can ill-afford to forego realizing money on any work that you create. We are not unreasonable. We will pay you what you expect to make if you put this play on.'

'I don't know what I'll make.'

'What is the longest run you anticipate?'

'Not more than six months, assuming it to be a smash hit.'

'Then what do you think the box office receipts would be?'

'Your share as an author?' remarked the second man.

'Perhaps *** francs.' I named a huge sum.

'Double it.'

'Double it?'

'We'll agree to double that amount, if you'll agree not to put on that play or to publish it.'

'This is ridiculous!'

'Call us crazy if you like. You said *** francs?' And he opened a large briefcase filled with banknotes.

'Look, here, stop. I cannot do this. I won't accept your money.'

'You agree to stop this project for nothing?'

'No. I don't agree to anything. I wrote this play and, call it vanity if you like, I intend to see it performed.'

'That cannot be.'

'We won't allow it.'

They were very excited and speaking at almost the same time. Chirping together like angry blackbirds.

'I don't think you can stop me,' I said.

'We don't wish to make you angry. We are trying to approach you in a friendly way.'

'Why is it you do not want me to have this play

performed?'

Silence.

Finally, I said: 'I am going to open my own theatre. I've been planning to do it for a long time. Now, I have sufficient funs to do it.'

'And you intend to stage the vampire play at your own theatre?'

'Yes.'

'I see that we cannot reach an amicable accord. So it comes to this: if you put that play on, we will ruin you.

'Who is we?'

More silence.

'I think I know who we *is...'*

'If you do, beware. Beware, Monsieur Dumas!'

'You'll be forced into bankruptcy.'

'We'll see.'

'Dishonored, you'll have to flee to Brussels in the dead of night.'

'Worse things could happen.'

'Worse things will.'

'What do you mean?'

'In plain language, we'll be revenged on you.'

'Indeed?'

'You have friends you love. Beware for them!'

'Get out! Get out now before I throw you out!'

'We don't make idle threats, Monsieur Dumas. We came here hoping to arrange things to everyone's satisfaction. We offered you a fortune...'

'The blame rests on you,' added the second man.

They left..

'Joseph,' I told my valet. 'If those two men ever come here again, do not admit them on any pretext whatsoever.'

Well, I soon had my theater, and after producing

several other plays, I was ready to stage Le Vampire. *This time, I received a visit from a beautiful woman.*

'Monsieur Dumas?'

'Ah! I cannot believe my good luck. The famous Baccarat!'

'You recognize me?'

'Yes, to what do I owe the honor?'

'I won't beat around the bush, sir. Would you like me to become your mistress?'

'I should be most honored.'

'There is only one condition...'

'I'm sure it is one I shall find delightful to fulfill.'

'You must give up all thought of producing that play...'

'What play?'

'The one about vampires.'

'You agree to be my mistress on the condition I give up staging Le Vampire*?'*

'That's it.'

'Who put you up to this?'

'That doesn't matter Don't you find me charming?'

'Very, but...'

'What do you care about that old play for? Men have fought duels for me, and all you have to do...'

'...Is the one thing I cannot do.'

'You won't?'

'No, I won't.'

'Then look out. And Marie Dorval, too.'

'Marie? What has Marie to do with this?'

'Nothing, except they know you love her, and–and it would be a shame if something happened to her, wouldn't it?'

'Baccarat, I don't know much about you, except by reputation, but I cannot believe you would let yourself

get involved in something like this,'

Baccarat looked rather confused, mumbled some excuses and left.

Now I remembered. *Le Vampire* was produced and was a considerable success. But soon thereafter, my father's creditors became nervous, started demanding payment and there was a kind of run on the bank. An English baronet was the leader of the group. I went to Sir Williams on my father's behalf, but the Baronet was very cold and refused to accept the reasonable compromise that I was offering.

"We want all or nothing," he said. "We are not going to be put off with words or partial payments."

I told my father: "Father, they're implacable."

"So be it," he responded. "I expected they would be. They want to ruin me–money is no object to these fiends, these bloodsuckers."

I remember his words and tone at the time. I thought he was just letting off steam. But now I realize he was never using words more precisely.

"I'll go to Brussels," he added. "I have no choice. If I write something. I'll send it to you and you can publish it in your name. Just send me the profits."

"All right, father."

He left that night.

A few months earlier, Marie Dorval had died in abject poverty. The famous actress who had created so many great parts, including ones in my father's plays, had been his lover. His lack of funds made it impossible for him to help her. He had to appeal to Victor Hugo to pay for her funeral. My father was unable to hold back tears as he pronounced the eulogy.

"They killed her!"

"Who, father?"

"The vampires!"

"What vampires?"

"Never mind–you wouldn't understand. But they killed her to hurt me!"

I returned to my father's manuscript:

It was with great difficulty that I kept my hands off this creature that had been responsible for the death of my beloved Marie Dorval; I longed to pull him apart. But the entretien *began.*

'So, now we are alone, Sir Williams.'

'So, now we are alone, Monsieur Dumas.'

'You killed Marie Dorval.'

'Marie Dorval died in hospital of natural causes, as I've read in the papers, in destitution. Her death had nothing to do with me.'

'Nothing! You sucked her dry. You sent Baccarat to seduce her.'

'Baccarat is very alluring–it's true.'

'And poor Marie liked women as well as men.'

'A fatal weakness.'

'You killed her!'

'Have it your way.'

'And you killed Marie du Plessis.'

'Your son's famous light of love died of consumption, everyone knows that.'

'I know better. You killed them both. To hurt me.'

'Actually, the Du Plessis woman was asked to seduce your son and convince him to make you forget about vampires. But she fell in love with him.'

'You don't stop at anything.'

258

'You were warned.'

'I've spent my time profitably in Brussels.'

'Have you? That's good to know. Look here, you refused to cooperate and we sanctioned you for it, that's all. We're not disposed to carry this little vendetta any further.'

'No? Well, I am.'

'What do you mean by that?'

'I mean that I've been tracking down your whole organization in Paris. I've got proof about you, Lord Ruthven.'

'My name is Sir Williams.'

'Is it? Records indicate otherwise.'

'Well, perhaps so—what of it?'

'You're a vampire So is X*** and so is Y*** and the rest of the names on this list.'

'But there's nothing you can do about it. It's not even illegal to be a vampire.'

'No, but it's illegal to commit murder and you've committed several.'

'Marie Dorval? Marie du Plessis? You'll be laughed at.'

'No, I mean the ones you committed for money to-gether with your human accomplices.'

'Whatever for?'

'Why, for the money.'

'If I'm a vampire what need have I of money?'

'You need money because your original hoard of gold would long ago have run out, if you hadn't found means of replenishing it.'

'Join us, Dumas.'

'Join you?'

'We can make you rich again, richer than you were before. A man like you can go far—especially with our backing you–you've seen what we can do to hurt you, but we'd rather not harm you. We need people like you–people with charisma, people with go.'

'Very tempting but I don't trust you.'

'Why not? We are really easy to deal with. We are in a delicate situation. We need anonymity, and access to human blood for food. We have no desire for notoriety or personal power–we just want to live peacefully among you.'

'Peacefully, you call it? Why did you kill Marie du Plessis?'

'The girl your son loved and called Camille?'

'Yes–what was the reason for that murder?'

'Don't use such highly charged and emotional word, I beg you. Camille, or to be more correct, Marie, was one of us.'

'She was a vampire?'

'Yes, in her early stages of development. She gave great promise. We wanted her to seduce your son...'

'Why?'

'To influence you. We knew of the great love that existed between you and the boy. If he could be persuaded to dissuade you from producing the play...'

'Well, she succeeded in luring my son into her clutches. He was really mad about her.'

'The trouble was, she was mad about him, too. There's nothing as unreasonable as a vampire in love. She couldn't be trusted. We were afraid she would reveal everything to him–which would be worse–so she was terminated.'

'You killed her!'

'Not exactly. She had tuberculosis, and...'

'Bah! The girl was young and strong as a horse. She might have lived for years, possibly even survived.'

'It's true. But unfortunately, she lost a lot of blood, which weakened her and she succumbed.'

'Weakened–you weakened her, you sucked her blood!'

'Just enough so the disease would kill her. We didn't do it ourselves. We have a clean conscience on that score.'

'Conscience!'

'It's a figure of speech.'

'There can be nothing but war between us, between me and all your kind.'

Williams, Ruthven or by whatever name you choose to call the creature, suddenly snarled and flew–I mean literally flew at me.

'I'll not put up with your insolence any more, Dumas. I'll show you what you get for crossing a vampire!'

I punched him full in the face. He staggered and fell down.

'You've broken my tooth, you bastard!'

'I'm no bastard.'

'Pardon, your father was–'

'Save your insults.'

Williams got to his feet holding his broken tooth in his hand.

'You know, you're awfully strong for a human.'

'My father could hold his horse between his legs and do pull-ups.'

'Really? Yes, I've heard of that.'

'Care for some more?'

'I'd like to kill you!'

'No doubt you'd like to suck my blood.'

'Oh, as to that, no. Just kill you. You're not the type whose blood we like.'

'Do vampires pick and choose?'

'We're very picky. Like mosquitoes. The best blood is that of a young virgin. In general, women are better tasting than men, young women better than old, blondes preferable to brunettes.'

He kept looking at his tooth. His own blood for once dribbled down his face.

'I really have to do something about this tooth. You'll pardon me. Rocambole!'

'A young man entered who I immediately recognized as one of the two men who several years before had come to bribe me not to produce the play.'

'Sir!'

'Get me some ice–this hurts. I'll have to see a dentist.'

'Right away, Sir Williams.'

'What do you propose to do, Dumas?'

'I told you. I'm going to expose you. And the other bloodsuckers on this list.'

'Permit me to say you cannot do that.'

'Are we going to start that again?'

'I'm merely pointing out that no one will believe you.'

'That you are vampire?'

'Yes.'

'Possibly. But I've thought of that. I have proof of the murders you committed to obtain inheritances. People may not believe you are a vampire, but they will easily believe you are a murderer.'

Rocambole returned with the ice which Sir Williams rubbed against his cheek.

A toothless vampire. People would laugh.

Suddenly, calculating his chances, he rushed at me again.

'You won't have any teeth left if you keep this up.'

'You're the only human I've ever met who was stronger than I am.'

'Too bad it didn't happen sooner. We've established that you are no match for me and that I have the power to expose you.'

'What do you want?'

'I want you to get out of France, you and all your friends, and Rocambole and Baccarat and all your human henchmen.'

'And if we don't, you'll expose us?'

'Yes.'

'You cannot kill us, you know.'

'I can put a stake through your heart and see if that works.'

'Bah! You'll be charged with murder, and one of our henchmen will come around, remove the stake, etc. Meanwhile, you'll be charged with murder.'

'I've thought of that. Which is why I'm proposing that you leave France.'

'Leave France! But it's so nice here. I really love Paris and the French countryside.'

'Go to England, go anywhere you like. I don't wish you on anyone, but you cannot stay here.'

'All right—we'll go.'

'You speak for all your brood?'

'Yes.'

'And don't ever come back.'

As I read these pages, a thought too horrible to contemplate occurred to me. If Dorval had become a vampire, and if she and my father had been off-and-on lovers over many years, might not she have–? And even I, I remember Camille–Marie always liked to nibble– what if?...